I0663257

Antelope Sky

Stories of the Modern West

Books by John D. Nesbitt

For the Norden Boys
Lonesome Range
Black Hat Butte
Red Wind Crossing
Rancho Alegre
Raven Springs
Coyote Trail
Black Diamond Rendezvous
Man from Wolf River
Not a Rustler
West of Rock River
North of Cheyenne
Poacher's Moon
Adventures of the Ramrod Rider
A Good Man to Have in Camp
Keep the Wind in Your Face
Shadows on the Plain
Field Work
Blue Horse Mesa: Western Stories
Antelope Sky: Stories of the Modern West
Seasons in the Fields: Stories of a Golden West

Two Novellas:
"Dead for the Last Time"
"Trouble in the Labor Camp"

Antelope Sky

Stories of the Modern West

John D. Nesbitt

SPEAKING VOLUMES, LLC
NAPLES, FLORIDA
2017

Antelope Sky: Stories of the Modern West

Copyright © 1997 by John D. Nesbitt

All rights reserved. No part of this book may be reproduced or transmitted in any form or by any means without written permission of the author.

ISBN 978-1-62815-697-3

for Antonio Pérez

Acknowledgments

The Prologue appeared in *Range of Respect*, a radio program produced by the Wyoming Chapter of the Nature Conservancy; reprinted in *Tumbleweed* (Morrill, Nebraska), Nov. 1996.

"In the Land of the Bucking Bronco" appeared in *West Wind Review*, Spring 1988.

"Junior's Family" appeared in *West Wind Review*, Spring 1989.

"Out of Bounds" appeared in *Wyoming Writing 1989*.

"Lodgers in Queer Street" appeared in *American Literary Review*, Fall 1991.

"Orin's Saddle" appeared in *Acorn Whistle*, Spring 1997.

"He Knew It, Too" appeared in *West Wind Review*, 1992.

"Pearl, Shadow and Light" appeared in *Wyoming Writing 1992*; revised and reprinted in *VeriTales: Note of Hope* (Fall Creek, Oregon: Fall Creek Press, 1993).

"On the Wind" appeared in *Wyoming Writing 1995*.

"All Our Neighbors Have Blue Lights" appeared in *Owen Wister Review*, Spring 1990; reprinted in *Letter from Wyoming* (Cheyenne: Wyoming Arts Council, 1991).

Seven of these stories have won awards with *West Wind Review*, *Owen Wister Review*, Wyoming Writers, and the Wyoming Arts Council.

To the editors and judges of the above publications and organizations, I would like to express my appreciation for their recognizing and encouraging my work.

This collection was first published in 1997 by RR Productions, copyright John D. Nesbitt.

Table of Contents

Prologue

The world at ground level is still in shades of grey—buffalo grass, sagebrush, and fence posts. In a few minutes the sun will rise, the sky will pale, and the world will emerge in color; but for the moment, the hue of the range land runs from dark to drab to pale and back to drab.

Above the low hills to the east, the first skies of morning come alive in deep vermilion, rays slanting upward to tinge the underside of a grey layer of cloud. The panel between hills and cloud takes on an even flush.

The ruby sky lasts for several minutes, then gives way to a lighter pink, and an orange, and then a golden flood that lights the land.

I take a broad view of the landscape. To the west I see four antelope, their saffron-and-white shapes a little brighter than the grass. As the day grows a minute older, the white becomes brilliant. One antelope has its rump toward me, while the other three graze in profile.

If I have my way, our lives will come together, one of those antelope's and mine. But I am in no hurry as I sit, my back against a fencepost and my rifle across my lap. The cold breath of morning—always coldest at sunrise—brings the smell of sage and dust and curing grass. These are the moments that live with us, the fragile moments when the world is new all over again—broad and spare, but rich in its spareness as the range land brightens beneath the antelope sky.

In the Land of the Bucking Bronco

He awoke to a world of grey and cold. As he emerged from jumbled sleep and undefined dreams, things of the world began to present themselves. He knew again that the crackly surface he shivered on was the upholstery of his pickup seat. The grey rectangle in front of him, with the silver button that would be cold to the touch, was the flop-door of his glovebox. Up and around, like three walls, rose the windows, grey on the inside from a coat of snow. Maybe it was bright and fluffy on the outside, but inside it was dull. If there was an idea, or a way to put in a picture-word the dry and throbbing sensation that spread from his skull to his throat, that would be grey, too.

His head was downhill, and he remembered why. The right front tire was flat, and he had had his choice of sleeping with his head downhill or behind the steering wheel.

The throb of his head recalled the beer he had drunk in Edgemont, South Dakota. A few miles this side of the state line, the tire had rumbled flat, and he had limped, or rather rattled, to the crossroads. The service station, restaurant, and bar had all been shut down, dark and cold in the falling snow. And so he had gone to sleep, head downhill, in Mule Creek Junction, Wyoming.

Now he was awake in the same place, trying to shrink smaller into the center of his warmth and knowing that he couldn't lie here long. He hoped that the restaurant was open by now and that the restroom was warm.

By the time the pancakes came, his hands had warmed and had become capable once again. Why, he wondered now, hadn't he gotten the sleeping bag out of the back, or the gloves out of the glovebox? Like the tire, they had seemed too difficult. Now, with the second cup of coffee, the task of changing the tire was seeming possible again. He hoped the rim wouldn't be scalloped when he went out to look.

As he tossed the flat tire into the tail end of the pickup and turned toward the restaurant, where he could wash his hands and order a cup to go, his eye caught the flash of green from his license plate. Iowa, green with white letters, looked from a distance like Colorado. That would never do. As soon as he found a job, he would apply for plates with the brown figure of a bronc rider against a background of white.

Later that week, not far from the Oregon Trail—in a valley of wheat, alfalfa, corn and beets, all flanked by pastureland and bluffs, cattle and horses, antelope and mule deer—in a roadside café called the Wagon Wheel, he found a job. Not cutting hay, or punching cows, or busting broncs, but a job all the same. He washed dishes and cleaned the kitchen for three-and-a-half an hour, and he could have a steak every night for supper. As Tiny, the owner/cook put it, that was better than getting poked in the eye with a sharp stick.

After about a month, one night when the grill was scrubbed and the chopping block was bleached, Tiny reached into the stainless steel upright cooler and into a brown paper bag. He took out two bottles of Coors, which he twisted open.

Tiny made small talk about the cooking and commerce of the day, and his hired man talked the same about washing dishes.

After a thoughtful sip, Tiny gazed at the bottle and then at the young man. "Well, Brent," he said, "I see you got rid of those Iowa plates. Does that mean you plan on stickin' around?"

"Yeah, I expect to stay in Wyoming a while. And the tags are cheaper here."

"You didn't care for the living back there?"

"I got tired of feeding hogs and cultivating corn for my old man."

"So now you're washing dishes."

"Not forever. I would've been feeding hogs forever."

"How long do you plan on staying here? —not that I'm worried. You're doing fine, as I told you the other day, but I don't expect you to stay on forever."

"Oh, I imagine I'll stay till I get a good idea about where to go next, and enough money to get there."

After a moment's pause, Tiny said, "I went out on the world once." He took a swallow and launched into his story. "It was twelve, thirteen years ago. Twelve. I wanted to go to Texas, work on the shrimp boats. See the ocean. A friend of mine's brother had done it, and made a bunch of money at it. Or at least said he did."

"Where'd you live then?"

"Just north of Fort Laramie. And I got my first lesson before I left town."

"How was that?"

"I stopped to fill up with gas when I left town. I had a '56 Pontiac, good car. I'd never driven south of here by myself, had hardly been out of the valley at all. When I was getting ready to pull out, I asked the fellow in the service station if it made any difference if I went through Torrington or Wheatland to get to Cheyenne. That guy just looked at me, and my car, and loaded up his lip with chew, and he said, 'Not to me.'"

Brent laughed. "That's pretty funny."

"Yeah, but I didn't realize at the time how true it was."

"So did you get to Texas?"

"Oh, yeah, I damn sure did. I got almost to Oklahoma City before I went broke. Sold my car in a little town called Guthrie, and then rode the bus on down to Corpus Christi. I piddled my money away wandering through those gulf coast towns, and no one was hiring on the shrimp boats. I ended up wandering the streets of Houston, being broke and hungry and damp and cold." Tiny lit a cigarette. "It was a lonely feeling to be far away in a big town, with no friends and no money and nowhere to go and nothing to eat. It's depressing. You wonder what the hell you're going to do, where you're going to get something to eat, how you'll ever get home. Because you want to go home then."

"I was cold the first night in Wyoming," Brent said. "That late snow we had."

"Were you broke?"

"No." Brent took a swallow, then asked, "How did you get back?"

Tiny flicked his ashes. "About like you. I got a job in a restaurant. That kept me warm and well fed, and after quite a little while I had enough to get home on. But I never forgot the feeling of being broke and hungry with no place to go. It makes your feet sorer and your legs tireder than they would be otherwise. You just feel hollow all the way down."

"I hope I never get that bad off," Brent said, picking at the beer label.

"Maybe you won't," Tiny answered, "but I don't suppose anyone could tell you a damn thing at this point, anyway." He went to the cooler and brought two more beers.

"How about you?" Brent asked. "How do you like the living now that you're settled? Are you happy the way you are?"

"I heard that one sure way to keep from being happy is to ask yourself if you are. Hell, I don't know. I've got a decent living, a decent woman, a decent place to live. I can go to Denver or Casper or Deadwood just about when I please, and I can pay for what I break."

"How long have you been married?" Brent wondered about Leona, the woman with a full head of hair, a full blouse, and a full pair of Wranglers. Sometimes she worked in the kitchen, but most of the time she was coming from or going to her horses. She was supposed to be one hell of a barrel racer.

"We're not entirely married," Tiny answered. "We haven't gotten around to it yet. But we've lived together about three years. She went to Arizona one winter to visit her sister, and she had me take care of her cat while she was gone. We'd been going around together a little less than a year. Well, after a few days of feeding her cat, I just said the hell with it, and moved all her stuff into my place. Been that way ever since."

"It's that easy, uh?"

"Sure. Nothing to it. You'll find out for yourself."

* * * * *

About a week and a half later, a little before closing time, two cowboys sat down to cheeseburgers and French fries. They were about Brent's age, maybe a little older— early to middle twenties, anyway. While he was waiting to take their plates, he visited with them. They were from up around Worland, between there and Ten Sleep. They had come down to Casper for a new pickup and had come over east here to enter a few rodeos. Tomorrow they were going back through Casper and up for a few ropings and rodeos around Ten Sleep, Basin, Greybull, and Lovell. They invited Brent to meet them for a few drinks after work.

As the three of them took turns at the pool table, Brent chatted now with Larry and now with Duane. Larry roped the heels and Duane roped the head. Duane said Larry was a mighty fine heeler, and Larry said, separately, that Duane was a bulldoggin' fool. Brent asked what else they did, and Larry said sometimes he entered the bronc riding.

"No," Brent clarified, "I mean, what else do you do besides go to rodeos?"

"We work," Larry said. "Both our families have ranches."

"Yeah, we work," Duane said, "but as damn little as we can get away with." He laughed, pushed a wedge of chew into his lip, then offered the can to Brent.

"No thanks. How often do you go to these rodeos?"

"Oh, three, four days a week, for the next little while here," Duane answered. "Your shot."

As Brent got up to shoot, Duane ordered whiskey and coke for Larry and himself, and a beer for Brent. He drew a checkbook billfold out of his boot, pulled out a twenty, slapped it on the bar, and tucked the billfold back into his boot.

Half a dozen drinks later, Larry was telling Duane that he was no kind of bulldogger, and Duane was telling Brent that Larry couldn't rope a fencepost and the only reason he rode broncs was he liked to eat dirt. Larry, with his hat tipped back and his thumb on his belt buckle, just laughed.

The pool game wore on. Duane, hand on Brent's shoulder, took to advising him on how to shoot his shots. On about the eighth drink, Duane offered him a job.

"Teach you how to run a hay baler," he said.

"Yer goddam right," Larry added, "and how to cut and brand calves."

"You know how to ride?" Duane asked.

"A little bit."

"Well, you got a job," Duane said, putting his left hand on Brent's shoulder and shaking with the right. "Let's drink to my new hired man," he announced, and he dipped into his boot for more whiskey, coke, and beer. "Hey," he called to the bartender, "give us another round here." And slap went another twenty.

With a couple of more drinks, the conversation wandered back to its earlier path. "You know how to drive tractor?" Duane asked.

"Hell, yes," Brent answered.

"Well, by God, you got a job." Then came the hand on the shoulder.

Brent, tiring just the slightest, said, "Well, really, I've already got a job."

Duane clapped him on the shoulder. "Well, now you got a good one."

The next day, Brent showed up early for the noon shift. Sitting at the counter, he gave the news to Tiny. "Looks like I'll be movin' on here in another week and a half."

"That so." Tiny's voice didn't express much of an opinion.

"Yeah, one of those cowboys offered me a job on his ranch startin' in a couple of weeks, as soon as they get back from all their rodeos. Up by Worland."

Tiny had a thoughtful look on his face as he wiped off the knife he'd been sharpening. "Them cowboys put sugar-plums in your head, uh?"

"What do you mean?"

"You think by and by you're gonna be like them?"

Brent drew back, just a little. So far, his image of his future self had been no more specific than sitting on a horse. "Well, yeah, they said I might go on the road with them sometime. But I don't see myself doing any rodeo tricks."

"Don't you see another difference between you and them?" Tiny studied the knife's edge and thumbed it.

Brent had a quick vision of Duane—calling the shots at pool, calling for drinks at the bar, driving a new pickup, offering people jobs—and it didn't fit his own self-image. But the tug was still there, the picture of being on horseback in the big wide open. "What do you mean?" he asked.

"It takes money to go off and rodeo and chase around and raise hell like those kind of cowboys do. Not all cowboys, but that kind." Tiny pointed the chef's knife at him. "You won't be a rambling cowboy, you'll be a low-wage worker just like you are now. You won't even be able to afford your own horse. You go up there and get stuck on a ranch, and your holidays'll be damn few." Tiny lowered the knife. "Until maybe they lay you off." He shrugged. "But like I said the other day, I doubt that anyone could tell you a damn thing at this point." Tiny turned and started shredding lettuce.

"Well, it'll be something different," Brent said. He spread out a road map on the counter and located where he thought the ranch ought to be. He was on the verge of wondering out loud if it made any difference whether he went through Worland or Ten Sleep, and then he checked himself.

Junior's Family

One evening toward the end of haying season, as I was setting up the new tent I'd bought, Junior came riding out to our place on his big sorrel. Just about the time I got the tent unpacked and rolled out, a brisk little breeze came along. I was fighting that when he dismounted, hitched his horse at the rail, and came over to help me.

"This your new tent, I take it," he said, stepping on a corner to pin it down.

"Yeah," I said, "it's supposed to be so simple that one guy can set it up in a storm."

He looked up at the sky, which was wide and clear and blue all the way up to the Bighorns. "Maybe you should have picked a better time to give it the full test."

"I can wait. I imagine I'll have plenty of chances to learn all its ins and outs."

"I suppose," he said, and then neither of us said anything more until we had the tent pegged out and poled up.

"I'll be right back," I said, and I skipped into the house to fetch a couple of beers.

"Let's check it out," I said, handing Junior his Coors and ducking into the tent. The smell of fresh tent fabric, sort of a blend of nylon and canvas and rubber, hung in the air. I unzipped the windows to let the place ventilate, and he crawled in to sit down. We each took a long pull of beer. I moved near the front flap and shook out a cigarette, while Junior dug out a can of chew. As I lit my smoke and blew a cloud out the entry way, Junior tossed an envelope onto the tent floor between us.

"What's that?" I asked.

"A letter."

"Who from? Some barrel racer from South Dakota?" Then I saw that the address was typed.

"Nope. It's from my family. My first family."

I could tell from the way he said it, so guarded, that he didn't mean his dad. "The hell," I answered.

"Yep." He leaned over and shot a stream of spit out the front of the tent. "My long-lost brother and mother." His tone was so deadpan that you couldn't quite call it sarcastic.

"Well, what do they have to say?"

"They want me to come and visit them."

"Where do they live?"

He picked up the envelope and half-showed it to me as he read, "Rancho Cordova, California. At least, that's my brother's address."

"Where the hell's that?"

"That's one reason I came over. To look it up in your atlas."

"I'll go get it. Wait here." While I was in the house, I grabbed two more beers and walked past my dad, who was smoking a cigarette and watching television.

"What's up?" he asked.

"Junior's here, and we're looking at the map."

"Oh."

It didn't take us long to find Rancho Cordova. It's in the suburbs of Sacramento. We looked over the route from here to there, finished our first beers, and opened the new ones.

"Do you think you'll go see him?"

"I'm thinkin' I ought to."

"When do you think you'd go?"

"That's the other reason I came over."

"Oh." We had been planning to go to the mountains, just the two of us, when haying was over. That's why my dad didn't think anything about us looking at the map. I was going to bring the tent, and Junior was going to set us up with his boss's trailer and another horse, plus his. Our plan was to check out some country we wanted to hunt in the fall.

"You see," he said, "Norm told me I could have this little vacation coming up. But I couldn't very well take that, and go to California, and still take off to go hunting later on."

"No," I agreed, "not when he's good about finding you work later on in the winter."

"And," he said, taking a sip of beer, "I didn't think your dad would favor you taking that much time off, either."

"Me?"

"Yeah, I wanted you to go with me."

"Oh," I said, letting it sink in. "That's the other reason you came over."

"Yep."

All the next day, while I ran the baler, I kept thinking about Junior. I remembered when he first came to stay with us. My dad was still working for wages, before he got my grand-dad's place, and we didn't have much money. Junior and I were friends at school, and his dad knew my dad well enough, I guess, to come and ask if he could leave a boy with us for a while. We lived in a little house in town then, and my dad sent my two sisters to the basement, and Junior and me out in the yard to play.

I have often wondered how it must have been with James Robert Henigan, Senior, a man with pride and dignity, when he had to come and ask another man to take his son for a while, so he could go on and find work.

I have also wondered what their conversation must have been like, with my mother leaning an ear from the kitchen.

I do know the outcome. Jim Bob, Junior's dad, came outside and said, "Junior, I gotta take off now. I got things fixed up so you can stay here for a while." He took a cardboard box out of the car and set it on the front steps. Then he kneeled down and hugged the boy and said, "Don't cry now, son. I'll either send for you or come back and get you." He got into his car, an old Plymouth as I remember it now, and drove away.

Junior didn't cry until we went to bed that night, down in my room in the basement, after my parents and my sisters had gone to bed in the two upstairs bedrooms. I cried, too, and I believed along with Junior that his dad would come back. Since then, it has seemed to me one of life's cruel jokes that a boy of eight would never see his father again, yet he was just old enough that he couldn't outgrow the name of Junior.

Also, as I ran the baler, I remembered an incident that happened after Junior had been with us about three years. We had just moved out to the ranch, and Junior and I were practicing roping a stump. A fellow about eighteen, who seemed really old to us at the time, drove into our yard and asked for Lucy, my older sister. Since I had the rope, Junior answered that she'd been fussing all afternoon and was probably waiting at a window. The young gentleman smiled in a smirky sort of way and walked up to the house. Lucy met him at the door.

"Your little brother said you might be ready," her beau teased.

"He's not my brother," she snapped. At seventeen, Lucy was just old enough to be ashamed of anybody in the family.

But it burned the hell out of me. I gave her the finger as they drove away, and I said to Junior, "You're brother enough for me." I wanted to hug him.

"It's my turn with the rope," was all he answered, but when I handed it to him he looked me in the eyes and said, "Thanks."

I never knew what happened to Jim Bob. When I was young, I imagined things I wouldn't dare tell Junior— things like his dad getting shot in a holdup, or running off with a rich and selfish woman, or dying while he was trying to save someone else. Junior never did ask, as far as I knew. As the years rolled, by I quit asking my parents.

On the morning after Junior had gotten the typed letter, I told my folks about our change in plans. My father joshed me about all the creeps in California, and what a bad influence they would be. My mother asked me what I thought about it, and I said I really didn't have much of an opinion. I would just go along with whatever Junior felt.

That evening, after I'd come in from baling and had a bath and sat down to supper, I asked my folks if they had ever heard anything on Jim Bob. It took me quite a bit of nerve to ask.

My mother answered first. "Yes, we did."

My dad looked at me and said, "But it wasn't anything to tell a boy. And then later, it seemed just as well to leave it sleep."

"I'll probably find out in California, if Junior hasn't already found out."

"Yes, you probably will," my mother said, giving in the first step.

"Is there any harm in my knowing before? I mean, I might be a little more prepared."

"Honey, do you promise to let Junior find out from his own relatives?"

I balanced a forkful of meat loaf at the edge of my plate. "O.K. That's a deal."

My mom looked at my dad, who cleared his throat and said, "Jim Bob died."

I met his eyes and said, "That's sort of what I figured."

My father went on, as if to get it over with. "It wasn't good. He was driving drunk. There were a couple of other people killed, too."

"When did it happen?"

"Not too long after he left here," my mother answered. "It just wasn't anything to tell a young boy, like your father said."

"I can see that," I agreed. After thinking on it a bit, I asked, "Why didn't these other relatives ever get in touch? Or did they?"

My dad answered. "No, they didn't, and I don't know why. Maybe they didn't try very hard. Jim Bob and the mother separated pretty unfriendly. Then again, maybe they did try. Wyoming eighteen years ago was even farther from California than it is now."

"I see. Did you ever try to get in touch with them?"

"Not really." My dad paused, then went on. "I sort of gave Jim Bob my word that I wouldn't make the first move."

"Oh."

We ate for a while without speaking, and then my dad wrinkled his brow, adjusted his eyeglasses, and said, "Well, it ought to turn out to be a pretty interesting trip."

"You can say that again," I answered, but of course he didn't.

* * * * *

The new tires on Junior's pickup had a road-whine to them, especially with the windows rolled down, so we had to play the tape deck pretty loud. By the time we got out on the desert past Salt Lake, we had played all the tapes once and some of them twice. Another way of measuring it was that we were six roast beef sandwiches and a complete chicken, cut up and fried, away from our little place on the fork of the Powder and from my mom, who had packed the food and told us to drive safely. Yet another way of measuring was to read the road signs—then add from Elko to Winnemucca, Winnemucca to Reno, Reno to Sacramento, and a few more to the brother's house. Call it 580, getting fewer at the rate of a little more than one a minute.

At the Utah-Nevada line, at the town of Wendover, we stopped to take a break and play slot machines. The one-armed bandits paid off just often enough to string us along, and after an hour we gave it up.

"I guess it's my turn to drive," Junior said. "You feel like travelling some more?"

"Sure. I'm not tired yet."

"Think we should get some beer?"

"Might not hurt at this point," I said, lying. I had told myself we wouldn't get into any trouble with drinking and driving on this trip, partly for my mom's sake and partly because I was haunted by my thoughts of what had happened to Jim Bob. But I couldn't come right out and say that, so when we got into the cab, I said, "If we start getting drowsy, we can pull over and catch some sleep."

"I imagine," he said. "I doubt we'll make it all the way to-night."

At the on-ramp to the interstate, we saw a hitch hiker. Junior pulled over for him. "I imagine we can stand some company," he said.

The guy was long-haired, long-jawed, and bearded, and he was wearing a cowboy hat. When I asked him where he was going, he said L.A. I told him to toss his gear on top of our tarp in back, and he could ride in front. Then I noticed he had a guitar, and I told him he could take it into the cab with him.

Once he was seated in front, I could see he was a little older than us, maybe thirty. He also smelled somewhat, which I figured was natural from standing in the desert sun. When I offered him a beer, he said he'd admire to drink one. Then he asked if either of us had a cigarette, so I pulled out my pack, gave him one, and set the pack on the dashboard. He was sitting on the passenger side because of his guitar, but we managed to introduce ourselves and shake hands all the way around. His name was Jack.

"We can't get anything on this damn radio," Junior said. "What can you play on that guitar?"

"Quite a few things," Jack said. "I reckon you guys like country tunes."

It struck me that he said "I reckon" for our benefit, since we were wearing our hats, so I answered, "I reckon we do."

So he plunked out "Your Cheatin' Heart" and "I Walk the Line"—no fancy pickin'—with Junior and me chiming in on the chorus. After that he did a long string of old standards, some of them shortened and some of them botched up in the wording. Then he asked if we'd like to hear "A Boy Named Sue," which neither of us had ever cared for, for obvious reasons, and I headed him off at the pass. "Can you do something of your own? Something you wrote?"

"Sure thing," he said. "I just happened to work one up on this trip. How about another cigarette, brother, and I'll bring it around."

"Help yourself."

He did, lighting it with the cigarette lighter. He strummed a few chords, twisted a couple of keys, and strummed some more. Then he opened up like this:

> *You are the pearrll of my mountain oyster—*
> *You are the apple of my eye.*
> *You are the cher-ry on my sun-dae—*
> *You're the one I'll love until I die.*

Jack smiled to us, took a puff on his cigarette as he strummed with his right hand, and picked up with the second verse:

You are the pearrll of my mountain oyster—
You are the ice cream on my pie.
You are the gray-vee on my French fries—
You're the one I'll love until I die.

He plinked around on the guitar for a few more seconds and then, with the cigarette in his mouth, came out with the third verse:

You are the pearrll of my mountain oyster—
You are the Swiss cheese on my rye.
You are the mustard on my hawt dawg—
You're the one I'll love until I die.

He strummed out a little flourish for a finale, and Junior and I gave him our applause. We were having a hell of a good time.

All this time that we were singing and laughing, though, I couldn't shake the thoughts that kept dogging me. For one thing, I had to admit that I was worried that Junior's real family, his real brother, might come between us. Also, I didn't feel quite right about keeping quiet on what I knew about Jim Bob. But I laughed and joked and sang along, wondering if Junior had any hidden fears of his own.

About an hour into Nevada, I had to take a leak, so Junior pulled over and I got out. From the tail end of the pickup, I could hear Junior telling a story and Jack laughing. When I got back in, Jack said, "Your partner was telling me about the time you broke your arm and he had to help you button up your pants for a while there."

"Actually, it was my wrist. That was the last time I ever entered the bull riding. My mom finally won that argument."

When we reached Wells, Nevada, we were running out of beer, so we stopped and bought gas too. I was looking at the map to see exactly where we were, and I had an idea. "Hey, Junior, look here," I said, tracing my finger along the map, "what do you think of turning north here, on the way back, turning at Twin Falls, and going home through Jackson?"

"Looks like we'd see some new country."

"Yeah. Let's keep that in mind."

Back on the road, Jack kept entertaining us with his stream of honky-tonk songs, repeating some he'd done earlier. After another hour, he said, "I think I'll give it a rest for a while," and he set his guitar on the floorboard, upright between his knees.

"When we get to Elko," Junior said, "I'd like to follow up on a tip I got from Mikey Dennison."

"What kind of a tip would he have?" I asked.

Jack must have picked up my sarcasm. "Who's this guy you're talking about?"

Junior answered. "He's a whistledick in our home town. He's been out this way a few times, and he told me how to find the cat houses in Elko. What do you think of stopping there for a while?"

"Sounds interesting to me," I said.

Jack didn't seem as interested. "I ain't goin' anywhere else. I can catch some sleep here in the cab."

It was nice to learn that the brothels in Elko were sure enough on the other side of the tracks and had red lights. There weren't any shady ladies walking the streets, though—the streets were quiet and deserted. Junior parked in front of a place called Sue's.

"You gonna stay here in the outfit, Jack?" he asked.

"Sure thing, brother. I've seen those places already. I'll keep an eye on things here."

"O.K. You comin', Jeff?"

"Might as well," I said.

We waited at the door for a lady to answer the buzzer and let us in, with a cheerful "Good evening, gentlemen." Then she went behind the bar.

We sat at the little bar and ordered draft beer, and when she said "Four dollars," I knew where the phrase "whorehouse prices" came from. Out of nowhere, a woman appeared. She was about thirty, in sort of a go-go dancer's outfit, leaning on my left elbow.

"What are you fellows up to tonight?"

"Oh, just sort of taking a look. I've never been in one of these . . . places before."

The madam bartender said, "Hell, you're in for it now. Once you been to a whorehouse, you're gonna have to try 'em all." She grinned, then curled her long tongue out to touch the tip of her nose.

"What's your name?" my friend asked.

"Jeff. What's yours?"

"Linda. Do you want to go to the room, Jeff?"

"I need to finish my drink."

"You can take it to the room, Jeff. You could be a gentle-man and buy me a drink, too."

"Let me think about it."

"O.K.," she said. "I'll go freshen up." I could see she didn't waste much time.

Junior meanwhile had stalled off his lady, and we nursed our beers. "What do you think?" he asked.

"I don't know. I guess a fellow needs to know about these things."

"Mikey says they get pissed off if you just come in and stall around and drink."

"I guess you're supposed to have made up your mind already."

"I guess."

About the time we were finishing our beers, Linda came out and started leaning on a guy who had just come in. He was down the bar a ways, so she had to raise her voice to say, "Let me check." She looked at me, raised her brows in a question, and I was hooked.

Back in "the room," after she had inspected me, she asked, sort of businesslike, "What way do you want it, Jeff?"

"What are my choices?"

"You can have a straight lay for twenty, a half-and-half for thirty, or a French for forty."

For once in my life, I wished I had listened to Mikey Dennison. I didn't know if a guy could bargain, so I just said, "I'll take twenty dollars' worth."

"Give it here," she said, and she took it out to give to her boss. Then she came back in, joined me underneath the skimpy little bed cover, put on a fine act of oohs and aahs, and next thing I knew, I was out at the bar again with Junior.

"Ready to go?" he asked.

"Yeah," I said, "but how about you?"

"I'm ready."

Outside I asked him, "Were you just setting me up?"

"Hell, no," he answered, "I wanted to try the colored place across the street that Mikey told me about."

A pale little lady, almost an albino, let us in the door. She called out, "Lay-deez!" and went behind the bar. As she served our drinks, a string of half a dozen girls came in, and our hostess said, "Would you gentlemen like to buy a drink for one of these ladies?"

Junior sort of winked at a girl in a red negligee, a girl the color of coffee and cream. She came over and put her hand on his leg, and they talked for a minute or so. I didn't look at any of them directly. Then Junior got up and left with his lady, and I was alone at the bar.

I was aware of a rich smell of perfume and softness against my arm. I looked into a very pretty and a very dark face. "What you-all up to tonight?" she asked.

"Well, I'm . . . uh . . . just in here on my friend's behalf."

"What about yoah behalf?"

"I was . . . behalfed just a little while ago."

"How long ago?"

"Ten, fifteen minutes ago."

"Oh, that like about a year," she said, running her fingers along my leg. I was thinking of ordering her a drink, to be polite, when she said, "Don' you wanna go to the room?"

"Nah, I'm just waitin' for my friend."

She drummed a farewell on my leg and was gone. Nobody seemed to waste time in this business. Before too long, Junior came out carrying his hat, walking casually with his lady friend.

"You come see me again," she said. He smiled, put his hat on, kissed her, and said he'd sure give it a try.

Back in the pickup, as we were rattling across the tracks toward the freeway, Jack nudged me and asked, "Well, how was it, brother?"

"Spent twenty dollars' worth of beer money," I answered.

Junior laughed. "Mine was only fifteen."

"It *is* a job," said Jack, lighting a cigarette, "that can be done by hand."

* * * * *

We slept under the stars out on the desert by Battle Mountain, and the flies woke us at about seven in the morning. We drove on to a truck stop, where we washed up and had breakfast. Hotcakes and coffee made me feel a little better, but I still felt tired and cruddy. I didn't see where either of the other two felt any better, but we all chipped in a comment here and there, telling truck driver and whorehouse jokes as we rolled across the desert to Winnemucca, on down to Reno, and then down through the pine forests and oak foothills to the hazy Sacramento Valley. Jack had put his guitar in back, so we listened to the radio. It was a long, hot day, and our driving shifts were shorter than the day before.

We parted company with Jack at a truck stop outside of Sacramento. He gave me one of those upright handshakes, hooking my thumb and wrapping his hand around the heel of mine.

"Nice travelling with you, Jack. Maybe we'll meet again."

"If we do," he said, "I'll buy a bottle of wine. Take care, brother."

We checked into a medium-priced air-conditioned motel room, showered, ate an early supper, and slept clear through till eight the next morning.

* * * * *

After breakfast, while I was showering just to get our money's worth, Junior called his brother and arranged to meet him at his place at four. That gave us the middle part of the day to kill, so we went to an air-conditioned mall to gawk around. We ate some pizza, shot a little pool, and played some electronic games. As we were putting our gear back into the pickup bed for the fourth time that day, Junior said, "I don't know how this is going to be. But I guess we're entered."

"I guess so."

"By the way," he said when we were in the cab, "they'll probably be calling me Jim."

I wanted to ask him at that point how he felt about the meeting. We had come all this way, singing and laughing and drinking and whoring, and really not said a word about the main order of business. I was one for getting things out in the open, while Junior, as usual, was playing things close to his chest. But I gave it a try. "Did they decide to call you that, or did you put 'em on to it?"

"I sort of put 'em on to it."

"Any particular reason?"

"I thought it might give me a better footing."

"Oh." I knew that his brother, who was a few years older, was named Bruce. I'd known that for years, but I didn't know anything more. I lit a cigarette and asked, "How's your brother Bruce set up?"

"Has his own business, as I understand it. Carpet wholesaler. Pretty well off."

"Married?"

"Uh-huh."

"Doesn't live with your mom, then."

"Nope."

"Are we going to stay there tonight?"

"Probably, if it's all right with you."

"Fine with me. How do you feel? About the visit in general?"

"About like climbing over the bucking chute onto a banana-horned bull." Junior looked at me and smiled. "But we're entered."

Bruce's house was in a nice neighborhood, with curvy streets and tile roofs, backyard pools and little courtyards. We walked over a tiny bridge that spanned a fake stream, with rocks cemented in it and water running. Junior hooked his finger into his lower lip, unloaded his chew, and spit out the crumbs.

Bruce answered the door, and my first reaction was that he looked like Junior—average height, square-shouldered, clear-eyed, clean-toothed—only made over. He had a full, trimmed mustache, hair neatly cut and layered, a tan polo shirt with an alligator on it, light blue bermudas, and sandals. He had an even sun tan and a deep, rich smile—deeper than Junior's, maybe from practice. He shook hands with his brother. "Jim! It's great to see you! Really glad you could come! Is this your friend? Jeff?"

Junior seemed awkward, almost over-powered. "Unh, yeah, this is Jeff. Jeff Tidwell. Jeff, this is Bruce Henigan. My brother."

We shook, each of us saying he was glad to meet the other. "We're out by the pool," Bruce said. "Let's go through this way." He led us through a shadowy living room, which seemed nicely furnished. We walked past a large built-in cabinet that held a television, a stereo set-up, hard-bound books, a few knick-knacks, and a wedding picture.

Out on the patio, I met the other person in the picture. "This is Janeen, my wife." She got up, a nice-looking woman about twenty-five, with a glossier tan than Bruce's. We were introduced all around, and Junior and I sat down.

I felt kind of funny, sitting in their webbed poolside chairs, with my right boot hiked up on my left knee, and my hat hanging on the toe of my boot. Junior had set his hat on a little table and was sitting up straight. We both drank Michelobs, while Bruce and Janeen drank Michelob Light.

The conversation fell into two halves, with Janeen occupying me with questions about our trip and the ranch. I couldn't follow Bruce and Junior's conversation, but occasionally I'd catch a word or two about work. Janeen was good at keeping me talking.

After a few beers, Bruce lit some coals and asked us if we'd like to swim. We both said no, and then he asked if we wanted to bring in our luggage. I offered to get it, and Junior stayed to talk with his brother. I couldn't get over how much they looked alike.

Janeen pointed out the room we would stay in, so I stowed our gear. When I returned to the patio, Bruce was saying, "And if you ever get tired of the weather out there, or want to try something new, I could fit you in pretty easily."

"Something to keep in mind," was all Junior said.

We made it through supper by asking what-all there was to do in their part of the country. There was plenty, it seemed, and plenty to talk about. Janeen asked how long we were staying, how much we wanted to see and do. I let Junior take the question.

"We don't have any real definite plans," he said.

"Just sort of . . . playing it by ear," Bruce offered.

Junior smiled. "Yeah. That's a good way to put it."

After supper, as we settled down in their living room, Bruce said, "Well, Jim, I don't really know where to start, you know, catching up on eighteen years. I guess I gave you sort of a sketch in my letter, but . . . I don't know . . . all the little things of a family . . ."

Janeen helped out. "Maybe he'd be interested in some photographs, Bruce."

"Sure. That's a good idea." He went to reach under the coffee table for an album, and stopped. "If you want to, Jim."

"Oh, sure. Bring 'em out."

There seemed to be a sudden relief in the air. Now there was a center to things. Bruce took up a chair between the armchair I sat on and the couch where Junior sat. With a little leaning, I could see the pictures as he turned the pages and explained. We saw the cocker spaniel Duke, followed by Bruce and Mom in the grade school years, Bruce in Little League,

Bruce and a stepfather who had been around for a few years, Bruce and his friends at high school graduation, Bruce and his college friends, Bruce and his carpet business, Bruce and Janeen on vacations—all of this with full explanations.

At about ten o'clock, the second album ran into blank pages, so I yawned and blinked my eyes and said I'd turn in. Janeen was rattling a few things in the kitchen.

Bruce looked at me and nodded. "Maybe Jim and I'll stay up a little longer and talk."

"Sure," Junior said. "I'm not sleepy yet."

Sometime after midnight, after I had dozed off, Junior came in and sat down on the other bed.

"How did it go?" I asked.

"I found out about my dad."

"Oh?"

"He died in Oklahoma. He's buried there."

"When did that happen?"

"Not too long after I came to stay with you folks. I sort of figured something like that had happened. He just wouldn't have left me."

"No, he wouldn't have." I didn't add anything, not knowing how much he knew or how much he wanted to talk about.

"Nice people, though, Bruce and Janeen. They made me feel comfortable."

"Hell, yes," I added. "You can't beat 'em."

"I have the second half of my visit tomorrow," he said, without any tone of joy that I could detect.

"How long do you think we'll stay here at Bruce's?"

"Just tonight, I think. What do you think of draggin' our freight after lunch tomorrow?"

"Sounds fine with me." Actually, I had gotten interested in some of the things they'd mentioned at supper, like San Francisco and the cable cars and the wharf and all of that stuff you always hear about. I went to add that maybe we could visit a ghost town up in the foothills, but I could tell by his light snuffle-snore that Junior was asleep.

The next morning I shaved for the second day in a row, which is rare for me. Bruce called in at work and stayed through breakfast with us. Janeen had already gone to work.

"Must be nice to be your own boss," Junior said, smiling.

"Sometimes." Bruce smiled back.

After breakfast, I loaded up our gear while Junior took leave of Bruce. They shook hands, exchanged a few words, and parted. Bruce waved to me. I waved back. "Come see us again," he called. I tipped my hat to him.

With all the things to do out there, there wasn't much to do between breakfast and lunch. We went to a sporting goods store to look at guns and camping equipment, and I bought a travel-size beer cooler for the return trip. We found a western store, where Junior bought a god-awful loud shirt, the kind that barroom guitar players wear, with fringes and a big button-up bib in front.

"What the hell you gonna do with that?"

"Wear it to lunch."

We had already agreed that I could miss out on their lunch, which was downtown. He left me off in the old part of town, across the river, which is restored in a historical sort of way with board sidewalks, all kinds of tourist shops, and restaurants with ceiling fans, brass railings, and frosted glass. It was a nice place to poke around in for a while. Down in a sunken courtyard I had lunch—a seafood salad and a schooner of really cold beer. I was pretty sure I was having a better time of it than Junior was.

At two o'clock, he came rolling up to the corner we'd agreed on. "Ready to go?" he asked, as I opened the door and climbed in.

"You bet."

He pulled out onto the freeway, which took us to another freeway, and before too long we were starting up the foothills toward Nevada. We stopped at a service station where they also sold beer, and we were on our way again. When I had settled the beer and ice into my new cooler, I handed one to Junior.

"Thanks," he said. "Thanks for coming with me, too."

"Any comments on how your lunch went?"

"The high point was when she offered to pay for my gas drivin' out here. I let her buy lunch."

"Not much fun, then."

"Not much. She made certain to tell me she had always cared for me, never quit worryin' about me." He cracked his can of chew on the steering wheel, then took a dip.

I lit a cigarette. "Did either of them give you any idea why it took so long for them to find you?"

"Not really. I didn't see any point in askin'."

"I guess not."

"It seemed as if it was Bruce's idea to track me down," he added.

"That makes sense."

"He's all right, he seems to me." Junior pushed his hat back on his head, took a swig on his beer, and said again, "He's all right."

We camped early that evening in the forest, still west of Reno. I got to set up my tent, which pleased me. We had sardines and crackers and cheese, along with the rest of our beer.

* * * * *

We highballed it across Nevada the next day, not stopping to gamble or go to the room or anything, except to buy gas and to eat. We made good time, turning north at Wells and going up to Twin Falls, where we saw the Snake River Canyon. That was worth the detour. From there we drove across southern Idaho, through potato country, and camped along a little stream in eastern Idaho.

We didn't drink all that day, but shortly before we camped that night, we bought some whiskey, ice, steaks, and canned beans. I set up the tent while Junior got a fire going and rigged up some willow spears to cook our steaks on. We ate our steaks with our pocket knives. Using the can lid for a spoon, Junior ate half a can of beans, and then I ate the second half. It was the best I'd felt since our first night on the road.

On our second drink, as we sat there gazing into the fire, I said, "Well, what do you think about that whole mess?" He hadn't said anything about it all day.

"Hell, I don't know," he said. "Take it all around, I think I like Bruce a little better than brother Jack."

"That's a nice comparison," I said. "I'd go along with that."

"But as for the other party, I can't say as I had any more feeling for her than I did for any of those women in Elko."

I thought on it. "That madam in the first whore-house seemed like a bad-natured bitch."

"Yeah," he said, "on second thought, that would be pretty even. But you didn't meet her."

"No." I knew which one he meant, even though he'd developed the talent not to mention her by name.

After a couple of more drinks, he went to the pickup, hauled out his suitcase, and opened it by the firelight. "Bruce gave me a whole slug of pictures," he said. "Here's one of him and me and my dad." He handed it to me, and in the soft light I could just recognize the three of them, Jim Bob kneeling, in someone's driveway. Like you see in a lot of old black-and-white pictures, the photographer's shadow got caught in the picture too.

"Bruce wanted me to send him some pictures," he said. "Maybe I'll send some of *my* family." He was sorting the pictures into two stacks, as if he'd carried them all this way and finally decided what to do with them. He took the bigger of the two stacks and tossed the bunch of them in the fire, where they curled up, smoked, and then blazed. I gave him back the picture I was holding. He added that to the little stack and tucked it into an elastic pocket of his suitcase. "I guess I know who my family is," he said, and he smiled in the fire light.

Out of Bounds

Down the slope from the stucco house, where the wheat grass and rye blew short green and long tan in the prairie wind, Benny turned out his goats. There they followed their goat pursuits—dancing, capering, playing king of the mountain on the irrigation headgate, and learning to jump the fence.

Together with his goats he lived on the fringe of cow country—on a hillside of grass and sagebrush, between alfalfa on the bench above and feed corn in the valley below. The land was cut by draws and washes, not fit for field crops, and it had been parceled into pieces too small to run any number of beef. It was the kind of place Benny could afford, and it seemed just the place for goats—even if this was cow country.

It was also just the place (across the fence) for the neighbor man and his brick house. He needed a little running room for his daughter's show horse, his son's dirt bike, the family dog, and the riding mower. There was also room for the wife's garden. Benny felt that he offended the man only mildly: by living in a house with a tin roof, by being Mexican, by having goats in cow country, by having female guests.

The neighbor, Hendrick by name on his little red barn of a mailbox, seemed to nurture some concern for Benny's solitude. One sunny Saturday afternoon, after he had sprayed the weeds along his driveway and around his satellite dish, while he was drinking his Lite beer and deriving satisfaction from burning the weeds along their common fence, Hendrick called out. "Looks like you got yourself some company."

From a harbored sense that the good neighbor didn't miss much, Benny glanced at the dirt road that ran from the stuccoed house to the paved road. He didn't see anyone.

"I mean your little pardners," the neighbor amended, with a tilt of the beer bottle in their direction. The goats were lined up along the fence, watching Benny as he hoed weeds.

"Oh yeah," Benny answered back, leaning on his hoe. "They're nice pardners."

"Kind of clever, aren't they?"

"In some ways."

"They've figured out that fence."

"Yeah, I know. They jump back in when I come home from work. I'll see what I can do about it."

"Oh, no trouble. We think they're cute. And my little girl's horse likes the company. Something about horses and goats— they make good company for each other." Neighbor Hendrick sprayed a shot of water where a fencepost was beginning to char. Benny wondered if the man's weed-burning would ever become so enthusiastic that he would have to water down his shake roof. A tin roof wasn't all bad.

"Do you like rhubarb?" It was Mrs. Hendrick, a trim figure of a woman in her late thirties. Benny had been aware of her in the background, tan in white shorts and halter top, as she worked in the garden. She held out a sheaf of red rhubarb stems with their broad, palmate leaves.

"I'm not sure that I've ever had any."

"Just cut up the stems and cook them with a little sugar and water. It makes good pies, too."

"Thank you." Benny moved toward the fence, took the bouquet of rhubarb, smiled at the lady, nodded at the man, and went into his house.

After that, he tried to keep in his goats. He tried tying them together, but they crawled through the fence in pairs. He tried hobbling them and after that shackling them to firewood chunks and old tires; they managed to kick and work loose. He tried running the fence a strand higher, only to teach them to jump better. And every day when he came home, there they came bounding and bunching up at the gate to meet their friend.

He was their friend because he fed them grain and kept them watered. If they had wit enough to pull cigarettes from his pocket, they were welcome to the treat. He danced with them, flourishing his arms like a symphony conductor and coaxing them up onto their hind legs where, satyr-like, they would stutter-step and pirouette.

Once he spent an entire morning in their paddock, where he contemplated their scaly horns, glassy bulging eyes, and velvet noses. He tugged on their beards, fiddled with their wattles, imitated their cud-chewing as they pushed their faces into his. He looked at their hooves from ground level. After sampling their grain, he drank from their trough, but not much.

He was their friend even as he planned to butcher the grown kids in the fall as he had done in other years and other places, then hang them in the lone cottonwood sheltering the house. Next he would cut and wrap the meat into careful packages to be stored in the freezer. He knew the goats inside and out, understood them in various ways.

Because he was their friend, he tried to keep them in. He patched and mended, but still they jumped his bounds. He was trying to come up with a new plan when the man across the fence lodged his complaint in his good country language.

The goats, cute little rascals though they were, chawed up the rosebushes and the wife's garden. Wouldn't bother him, you understand, and they didn't eat all that much of the horse's hay, but a man's got to keep peace in the family.

Of course.

Benny thought of slaughtering them before their time, but that would be wasteful and unfair. He thought of taking them to the sale, but there went all of the planned tacos and ribs and chops. He tinkered with the fence a little more in the evenings, to put on a show of effort and to buy a little time, to show with gestures what he wouldn't have put into words—that good neighbors try to make good fences.

Meanwhile, the goats were growing. They knew enough to come back to the pasture when Benny came home from work, but they didn't know that when their horns got just so long, they could push their heads through the hogwire mesh but could not pull back through. They did not learn. That's what got the little Toggenburg kid into trouble. And Benny, too.

* * * * *

Benny came home one hot and dusty day to find the Toggenburg stuck in the fence as usual. As Benny worked the head sideways back through the hog wire, his hand came back red from the brown neck. Slippery blood on the brown hand. A gash in the little goat's neck. Wet hair . . . dog slobber.

His first mistake was in telling the neighbors that their Samoyed had wandered and done wrong. The man said, as people in brick houses are apt to say, that their dog never left the yard, that one of the reasons they lived in the country was so they wouldn't have to keep their dog locked up.

Benny imagined the second remark was for his benefit, since he kept his spaniel in a pen. Well, then, he conceded, if the dog really didn't leave the yard, they must not have a problem.

Going home, Benny felt as if he had sat down in a game of checkers he hadn't been watching, and he had just made an unwise jump.

Benny did such as he knew how for the little goat, washing the wound with alcohol and rubbing it with ointment. Still the flies did their work, so that in a few days he found maggots. Benny washed them out with alcohol, rubbed the ointment in with even more hope, but the next day there were more maggots, widening the wound. By the next day, all that was left was to knock the young goat on the head with a crowbar—right behind the troublesome horns, scattering a few maggots on the way. He wished he hadn't mentioned anything to the neighbors.

There was recourse of a sort, but he was nearly out of moves. He penned the goats in close at night. He loaded his lever-action Winchester .22 and left it by the door.

It was a pale night, hard to sleep, the kind of night when a fellow could drive with no headlights. The goats were calling. Moonlight found Benny on his front steps, barefoot up to his mustache, lining up his rifle sights on a large white dog. His second mistake was shooting it in the flank instead of the head, allowing the Samoyed to return to the yard from which it never strayed. That meant, among other things, that he would now lose wages by going to court.

* * * * *

The judge was fair. He ordered Hendrick to pay the market price of a butcher goat, and he ordered Benny to pay the vet bill for the dog. He cautioned the dog's owner that if dogs got into trouble, that was the consequence of being allowed to run free. On the other hand, he admonished Benny that this was not the old West where men took Winchester justice into their own hands, that there would have been more justification had Benny not known whose dog it was, and as a lesser but not negligible point, that it was against the law to discharge a firearm at night.

Hendrick went back to his office to sell insurance and annuities. Benny, who had taken the afternoon off, went home.

* * * * *

The next creature to cross the fence, or more likely go around it, was pleasant Mrs. Hendrick, bearing a rhubarb pie in apparent truce. Benny invited her in. They sat at the kitchen table with the pie between them. She accepted the cigarette he offered.

"Don called and told me how things turned out in court," she began.

"I guess the judge was pretty fair. As fair as he could be."

"The vet bill is going to be more than the price of a goat."

"I probably shouldn't have shot the dog, but my goats mean a lot to me."

"I understand that. They're the only company you've got." A twinkle came to her face and she added, "Most of the time."

"Well, yeah," he agreed, smiling as he tapped his cigarette ash, "most of the time."

"How did you like the rhubarb I gave you before?"

"Just fine. I cooked it with sugar like you told me."

"This pie has raisins in it. I hope you like it."

"I'm sure I will." They sat quietly, each smoking, until Benny continued. "Shall I bring the pan back? The pie pan? When I'm done with it?"

"Oh, don't bother. That's one of those aluminum ones that you can throw out."

"O.K." Benny was aware of her crossing her left tanned leg onto her right, beneath the table as she shifted in her chair. If the pie plate didn't have to go back, he thought, then maybe her husband wasn't meant to be troubled by it.

It was mid-afternoon and the neighbor lady, whose name he learned was Connie, didn't seem to be in much of a hurry. They talked about the weather, how warm it had been and how little rain. Benny poured lemonade into tall ice-cubed glasses. They had another cigarette, and they talked about how, for a house with a tin roof, this wasn't as deathly hot as a person might expect.

They talked about his goats and how long he had been raising them. He explained that he bought half a dozen kids every spring and raised them until late fall. Then he told a story about some goats he had kept in the last place, the place he had rented before he had bought this one.

"I lived next to a Basque guy. You know they're really stuck on lamb. They think there's nothing like it. He was always telling me to get rid of my goats and get lambs instead. He lived by himself, like I did. Once in a while when he barbecued lamb, he'd invite me over, to prove how good it was."

"Was it good?"

"Oh, yeah. He would take about half a head of garlic, peel it, put it in a mug with red wine vinegar, mash it up with the handle of a butcher knife, and smother the lamb chops with that mess. It was strong, but it was good."

"But he didn't care for goats."

"Not really. He said they were too much trouble. A funny thing happened one time. We were having a pretty good rain storm, in late spring, and he called me up in the middle of the night. He spoke Spanish a lot better than English, but he always talked English to me. 'Hey neighbor,' he said, 'I think you sonofabitch goats under my house.' He had left the crawl space open to work on some pipes, and the goats had gone through the fence and gotten in there. They woke him up when they hit their horns on his floorboards, right underneath his bedroom."

"I guess that would make a person sit up and wonder."

"I think he kept money stashed in his floor some place, and he probably thought someone was trying to rob him."

"That's a pretty funny story."

"It's always seemed funny to me."

They sat for a few minutes more without speaking. By and by she rattled the melting cubes in her glass and said, "Well, I guess I should be going home now."

At the open doorway, as he stood with his left hand on the doorknob, she paused with her right hand on the other side of the door-latch assembly, with the door between.

"It was nice of you to bring the pie. Thank you."

"You're welcome. I didn't want you to hold a grudge against me."

"I wouldn't be mad at you."

"That's good. I wouldn't want you to." Her eyes twinkled as she smiled and let go of the doorknob. "Thank you for the lemonade," she said, and she walked down the concrete steps.

Benny stood at the window and watched her walk back around the end of the fence to her house. Then he went to the sink, let the water run until it was cold, and drank two half-glasses of water.

His father had told him to try to learn something, at least one thing, every day. As Benny set the water glass upside down in the dish drainer, it occurred to him that today he had learned that a fellow isn't always out of jumps as soon as he thinks he is.

Road Hunter's Neighbor

I see him come rolling in at a little after seven on a Sunday morning. It's dawn in early October. The street lights went off a little while ago, but the sun isn't all the way up and shining yet. The dark pickup, lights off, stands out in the grey of morning.

I call him Road Hunter—not to his face, of course, but when I mention him to my wife. I refer to him that way because I think he does a lot of his hunting along the roads in his pickup. When he comes in right after dawn this morning, I figure he's been out early and met up with something.

I'm sitting in the kitchen having a cup of coffee when he comes down the alley and pulls into his back yard. He doesn't have the back area fenced off or planted in lawn, so he can pull in and swing around, which he does. I see the rifle in the rack above the back seat.

Until I started observing Road Hunter, I hadn't paid much attention to how guys rack their rifles. It's sort of like noticing whether people hold the phone with the right hand or left—interesting to watch. As for rifles, most guys have the butt end behind their head, from poking it in barrel first before climbing into the cab. If two guys are in the pickup, the guns are pointing opposite directions, which is also better if the rifles have scopes. They fit better and don't rattle against one another. I know that much from experience.

Road Hunter often racks his rifle in the opposite direction, and quite deliberately, it seems to me. I've seen him lift it in from the driver's side and heft the butt end in first. My analysis is that he can get the rifle off the rack and into firing position without getting out of the cab. When he carries two rifles, he puts the quieter one, the small-caliber gun, on top, with the butt end on the passenger's side. The big caliber gun goes in on bottom, barrel end first.

Usually I don't see him load up the pickup in the early morning, which he must have done this morning. But I've watched him at other times. One afternoon about a week and a half ago, he loaded up when he got off shift at the sugar factory. He put the big rifle in by itself, in his favored style. When he came back about three hours later with a dead antelope, the rifle was pointing the other way. I guessed he must have finished the hunt when he was outside the cab.

This morning the rifle is in road hunting position, as I imagine it was when he left. I see that as he first pulls in. As he swings the pickup around and backs it toward his garage, I look hard at the camper shell but can't see through the tinted windows. The brake lights go on as he stops the pickup, then they go off as he gets out of the cab. He slams the door, goes around to the back, lifts the flap window, drops the tailgate, and drags out a mule deer with antlers.

He pulls the deer by its hind legs until he has it crosswise on the back of the pickup. Then he grabs the antlers and slides the body off the tailgate and onto the ground, where it lands with a flop. I think, he must be awfully strong to wrestle a big deer like that into the pickup by himself.

The lights are not on in my kitchen because I wanted to sit here with a cup of coffee and watch the sun rise. Now I can do that and observe Road Hunter as well. I don't think he would care if he knew I was watching. He's pretty nonchalant, and deer are in season now.

The buck is lying there with its tongue hanging out and its eyes dulled over, as dead deer always do. I have heard that game wardens, or maybe wildlife specialists (which is how most game wardens start out before they get into the police aspect of their work) can tell by the dilation of the eyes whether the animal was shot at night. I wonder if it's true, and I wonder how this one would check out. Maybe he had the first pink skies of the east in his eyes when Road Hunter got him in the crosshairs.

It doesn't look as if the deer has been field-dressed. Most hunters bring home their animals already gutted, so all they have to do is skin them. Sometimes Road Hunter does it that way, but other times, like now, he brings it straight home, as if he'd gotten it in a place that didn't lend itself to field dressing.

He goes into his garage and comes back out with the legs of a tripod, long pieces of black pipe. Next he brings the brace that holds the legs together at the top, and he sets up the apparatus, which requires a little dexterity, since the legs are about nine feet long. Then he hooks up his hoist, skins the rear hocks of the deer, sticks the cross-iron, or gambrel, into the hamstrings, and starts winching his animal.

His tripod is an interesting variation. Most people use a tree limb or garage rafters, but Road Hunter doesn't have trees in his back yard, and I would guess he doesn't want to make a mess in his garage. I think he's pretty meticulous. I've watched him pack and unpack for his various expeditions, and he's usually quite neat about it. When he comes home, he doesn't dump his binoculars, ax, camp stove, and tent in a big heap. He puts the stuff away as he unloads it, and he hangs his tent and sleeping bags to air out and dry. The pickup comes in muddy and bloody at times, but he always unloads it and at least washes out the bed. And as for dressing the deer out in the open, I don't think he is bothered by any sense of being watched.

After he has the deer hoisted upright, he starts skinning it with his bone-handled hunting knife. He peels and trims, rolling the grey hide down and exposing the white and purple of the fat and flesh. He does it all neatly and methodically with his shirt sleeves rolled up. It's frosty out there, and the steam rises from the hind quarters of the deer. I doubt that he thinks about what it means to take the life of an animal. He goes about it all in a workmanlike way.

He must be efficient with the butchering, too. Sometimes his friends bring over their own animals, and they have meat-cutting parties in the garage. They drink beer and laugh from seven till midnight—not as bad as the Monday Night Football parties that the last tenant used to throw, but rowdy all the same. They bone all the meat, it seems, because the next day his two black Labs are picking over the red-and-white remnants of skeleton.

This morning I see the two dogs—bird dogs—are watching from their pen. They know what's up. They can smell the warm promise of scraps.

He has the hide down below the shoulders now, and I can see the spread of bloodshot where he put a bullet through the front quarters. A quick kill, no doubt. He cuts around the neck,

John D. Nesbitt

finds a hacksaw in the back of the pickup, and separates the hide and head from the hanging body.

None of this is new to me. I've seen it all before, growing up in this town and being around hunters all my life. I even hunted when I was in high school, but that was a long time ago. My dad took me out and prodded me into killing my first deer. The next year I killed another and got blood up to my elbows, just like this guy is doing. Then, the same year I killed the second deer, we went out to hunt antelope in a late season, in November, and I shot one in the leg. It got away. Antelope can really move on three legs, and it stayed half a mile ahead of us until we lost it at sundown. That night the weather got cold, down near zero, and I imagined that poor suffering animal out on the cold prairie while I nestled in my warm bed. I was angry at my father, and I felt I had done something disgraceful. Maybe you could say I grew out of hunting after that. I hunt with a camera now.

I watch as Road Hunter tumbles out the intestines and then reaches down in with both hands and pulls out the heart and lungs. He trims away the heart and sets it on the tailgate. All of the innards are in a heap, steaming like the empty carcass. He slashes at the liver and lifts it free from the pile, cuts it in two on the tailgate, and leaving the knife by the heart, takes the two pieces of liver to the dogs.

Back at his work, he picks up the knife and returns to the deer. He trims away a few scraps here and there, and then with the stiff blade of the hunting knife, he opens up the breastbone all the way down to the neck. He nods and seems satisfied.

There's no point in arguing about whether it's right or wrong, with him or with anyone else. I'm familiar with all the arguments. Once when our daughter Bethany was little, she watched a neighbor working on a deer, and she asked if it had hurt. This was in our other neighborhood, but it was the same idea. The guy said no, it didn't hurt for long at all. That's one argument. Then there's population control, our place in the food chain, self-sufficiency, and the rest. They say that if you eat a hamburger you've helped kill a cow, and that hunters are honest enough (translate: man enough) to do their own killing.

Maybe so. But to me, regardless of the arguments, it comes down to one thing. It's crude. People like this one, Road Hunter, think they make everything all right if they pay for their licenses. They pay an agency that takes it upon itself to portion out the privilege of killing wild animals. Hunters pay so they can send a bullet through the body of a splendid creature like that one, and then they do what he's doing now.

This seems like the worst part, the ultimate violation. I watch as he uses the hacksaw to cut through the skull, once across the front and once behind the ears. He twists the antlers free and holds them out to admire them. It's a medium-sized rack, three points on each side. He takes the antlers to the garage.

My mouth is dry. I pour another cup of coffee. I decide not to add any milk because I don't want the refrigerator light to come on.

As I sit down again, I see him coming out of the garage and unfolding a white cloth bag. He shakes it out to its full length, slips the open end around the dangling front legs, and draws the bag up around the body. He tucks and wraps it around the top.

There's an odd sort of detachment to all of this as I sit in the grey kitchen with a window that lets me see but not hear much or smell anything. I think it might be interesting to smell the warm, liquid smells on the cold morning air, even if there was a dead animal cooling there. I don't move. I realize that I don't want him to know I've been watching, even though he clearly doesn't care.

He takes the knife and the heart into the house, the warm place where his live-in girlfriend has probably been sleeping all this time. After a few minutes he comes back out, clean-handed, rolling down the sleeves of his khaki shirt. The knife is in its sheath.

Now he loads the guts and the hide with its plundered head into the back of the pickup. He wipes his hands on his jeans, slams the tailgate, closes the camper shell, gets into the cab, and drives away. It's against city ordinance to put animal parts in the dumpsters, so I imagine that law-abiding Road Hunter will find some place to dump them in the country.

In the meanwhile, he leaves the deer hanging in his back yard, while I am here sitting at the kitchen table, gazing. The sun is beginning to brighten up the kitchen. I notice a splotch of red forming on the linen bag down by the shoulders of the deer. I imagine the bloodshot front quarter and I find the image disgusting. Repugnant. But I also know that I didn't mind watching.

How Firm the Price

Skip was taking the polished brass knocker off the front door when the phone rang for the first time. A lady with a middle-aged voice said she would like to see the puppies and said she would come right over. Skip gave her the address and directions with the screwdriver still in his hand, and he went back to his task.

The knocker had been difficult to mount, as he recalled, getting the holes lined up and drilled, cutting the lag screws just the right length, and making the connections. Taking it off was a three-minute job. He held it in his left hand, hefting it. The thing was heavier than he remembered. It had been a wedding gift from one of her old boyfriends, who had seen fit to have it engraved with "Skip and Andrea" on one line and "Welsch" below it. It was easy to think, at this point, that gifts done that way were not the best kind.

The phone rang a second time. A lady with a younger voice than the first one asked if the price was firm. Skip said pretty firm. She said she'd like to look at the puppies. He explained that another lady was on her way and that it might be better to wait about half an hour. The younger lady said fine, got directions, and hung up.

The middle-aged lady had dyed strawberry blonde hair, bifocals hanging from a chain, and an even distribution of extra weight. Skip didn't recognize her, and she didn't pay much attention to him. She went straight for the big cardboard box, leaned over, and started cooing and baby-talking. Skip set the puppies on the floor, and the little male with lopsided markings waddled over to the lady and started licking her exposed instep.

"Well, this is mama's little baby," she cooed, and setting her purse on the floor, she stood up, cuddled the puppy on top of her ample bosom, and let it lick her face. She puckered her lips and made smacking sounds, four or five of them, as she stared her little darling in the eye. "You just came running right up to me, didn't you? You want to come home with me and be mama's little baby?" She looked at Skip and said, "I can tell right from the beginning. This is my puppy."

Skip nodded. "He's a spunky one. His markings aren't as good as some of the others', but he's got character."

She held the puppy out for inspection. "He looks fine to me. I've had Springers before."

"Oh, I think he's fine, and if you've had Springers before, you know as much as I do."

"Well, I think I'll take him." Cuddling the puppy with her left arm, she bent at the knees and picked up her purse. "The ad said eighty-five. Will you take eighty?"

Skip hesitated. It was bad business to cut your price on the first pup, but the lady hadn't really taken pick of the litter, and the rest would look better as a group without this one. "This is the first pup," he said, "but O.K."

"Now are they papered?"

"No. That's why the price is so low. But they're purebred. You can tell that."

"Oh, no doubt about that. I know Springers."

"Uh-huh."

She dug into her purse. "Here's eighty."

"And I thank you. Would you like a receipt?"

"No, thank you."

"O.K. I hope everything goes fine for you and your puppy."

Then the lady was gone, and Skip put the other six pups back in with Dottie, who had watched the transaction with cocked head and not so much as a woof.

* * * * *

The second lady was several years younger than Skip, maybe twenty-five. She had straight, shoulder-length blonde hair, blue eyes, clear features, and a nice build. She was dressed in a light blue pullover V-neck and matching shorts, and she wore a wedding ring.

Skip put the puppies on the floor, and she knelt to play with them. Her loose jersey gave him an unexpected peek, which he took quickly and then looked away. Fetching a picture of the litter's father, he knelt on the floor beside the woman.

"This is the father," he said. "He doesn't have papers, but Dottie here does. But you can tell they're purebred."

The woman looked at the picture, at complacent Dottie, and at the pups. She nodded.

"Have you had a Springer before?"

"No, but my husband did when he was growing up, and he says they're great dogs."

"They are. Do you have kids?"

"Two boys, four and six."

"These are great kids' dogs."

She nodded as she teased and batted at the puppies.

"Does your husband hunt?"

"Not really."

"If he did, these are good hunters."

"Un-hunh. What's this one?" She rolled it over to see the whisker on its belly. "A little boy."

"Did you want a little male or a little female?"

"No real preference, really. Aren't they priced the same?"

"Oh, yeah, same price. It's just that some people don't like to bother with a female when she gets to breeding age."

"Oh."

"And other people don't like a male dog if they have little girls at home."

"Oh?"

He wrinkled his nose. "Their habits, you know, as they grow older."

She looked at him.

"The dogs' habits."

"Oh." Comprehension showed on her face.

"No harm in a male dog, though, especially if you've got little boys."

She smiled and stuck out her tongue at the puppy. "I like this one." But she didn't pick it up. Instead, she looked at Skip and said, "What's your bottom price?"

Skip, kneeling on the carpet close enough to touch her, felt warm and generous. What the hell, he thought. He'd already cut his price on the first pup, and he still had five to sell. "I don't know," he said, making eye contact. "Make me an offer."

Her mouth was barely open, and she moistened her lips with her tongue, as if in hesitation.

* * * * *

"I take it you're not married," she said, as Skip lit a cigarette.

"Not any more. What was your first clue? Not locking the front door?"

"No, using a dining room chair for a bedside stand."

"Good oak, though, don't you think?"

"Oh, very nice."

The atmosphere was cheerful, but it seemed to Skip that there wasn't going to be much more in the way of intimacy. "We just got things finalized a few days ago," he said. "I haven't gotten around to shopping for new furniture." He was tempted to add, *And I won't, either, if I keep giving puppies away.*

"Any kids?"

"No, no kids."

"That makes it a lot easier, I guess."

"I guess. That's what everyone tells me."

She rolled onto her side to face him, and she laid her hand on his arm beneath the sheet. "There's no reason you can't have any," she said. "You're still young, and good-looking, too."

"Thanks. That's nice to hear."

She patted his arm. "Didn't your wife want any kids?"

"We never got that far." He laughed. "I mean, to the point of actually having them."

She smiled. "Well, maybe you'll have some, some day. They're really worth it."

* * * * *

When the woman was ready to go and had gathered up her puppy, Skip asked her, "Are you happily married?"

She arched her eyebrows and nodded in a so-so manner. "Yeah, I guess you could say I am."

"Well, I hope everyone likes the puppy."

"Thank you," she answered, "and I hope everything works out O.K. for you."

Skip opened the door for her and watched her walk away. Maybe she was happily married, or something like it. She certainly seemed happy about her kids. Maybe she was just a little adventurous and liked to save money when she could. She probably meant it when she said he ought to be able to do all right for himself. Skip smiled and waved to her as she got into her car. He was happy for her, happy he'd given her the puppy. He was sure her husband and boys would like it.

Lodgers in Queer Street

The Ackermans were gracious hosts. I know it's a common phrase, but I really mean it. They could make a person feel like—well, like valued company, like they were glad you came. They served meals that clearly took more than the usual effort, good meals and not just frilly stuff. They didn't take a little piece of meat, spice it and sauté it and sauce it, and then hide it in a nest of vegetables with funny names. They served you off the platter. They served complete meals—no lasagne or enchilada casseroles, but the full Italian or Mexican layout, right down to the vino or Dos Equis.

They always had a good spread of drinks to choose from, even on Sundays, when the liquor stores are closed. You never had to ask for a drink, yet you never felt they were pushing the drinks. The Ackermans drank at their own pace and no doubt assumed that their guests could do the same.

Everyone came away from their house with the same impression. It was an easy feeling to be a guest there—the Ackermans never tried to get someone to stay longer, and they never gave you the feeling they were trying to get rid of you. There was only one thing to be careful about, and that was to call first. The story came from another couple, a State Farm salesman and his wife who weren't in town all that long, who met the Ackermans shortly after both couples had moved to town. They all got happy drunk together in the Red Hat Lounge, and the Ackermans invited them for dinner the next day. When they showed up, as the story went, the Ackermans weren't expecting them. They were apparently on the tail end of a weekend binge, not a pretty sight, and had forgotten about inviting the other couple. The State Farm salesman, as he told the story, made apologies about coming on the wrong night. So that's how the word got around to call first.

I knew them from when they first came to town. They had me in to work on their house. I knew the house from before the time the queery schoolteacher and his wife had it, and I knew they hadn't kept it up very well. So there were leaky faucets and bad electrical outlets and dead bathroom fans, the kinds of things I do along with my main line of carpentry. I got to know Warren better than Beverly. At the end of the second day, when all my handyman chores were over, I sat out on the patio and had a few beers with him. After that I'd bump into them in the bars, where I would have a drink with the two of them.

My first dinner invitation came about a year after I had first met them. I had heard so much about them that I had the feeling I'd been there several times before. Naturally, I called first, even though they'd asked me in the middle of the week, and it was only Saturday. I showed up with beer and red wine. Warren met me at the door, took my offerings, and ushered me into the living room. There he introduced me to a younger couple, maybe ten years younger than me and fifteen years younger than the Ackermans. Early twenties, I'd say, all scrubbed up but not very wealthy-looking. I didn't recognize them.

Warren went to join Bev in the kitchen, so the three of us sat and talked and drank Michelob. I remembered Warren serving it before, so that's what I had brought. In the course of the conversation, I learned they had just met the Ackermans the evening before, at happy hour. Originally from Wisconsin, they had been working in Rapid City and were on their way to Denver. They were having their water pump fixed when they met the Ackermans, who, being gracious hosts, invited them to stay. The girl's name was Renée, and the young man's name was Danny. They were both in restaurant work, and they didn't seem to be married.

When I first saw them, I wondered how I got matched up with them for dinner, but then when I found out they were sort of an afterthought, it made more sense. As I took the empties to the kitchen, I glanced into the dining room and saw the table set for five. No one else was expected, which meant the Ackermans had originally invited me by myself.

Dinner consisted of some small elk steaks, which had been given by a man whose property Warren had assessed; medium-sized lobster tails, which they bought in frozen lots when the seafood man came through town; sourdough French bread, which Beverly ordered and had shipped a dozen at a time from San Francisco; white wine, which they bought by the case in Colorado; and red wine, Almaden claret, which I had brought. There was also a spinach and lettuce salad, good tasting, but without a personal story behind it.

After dinner, as we were putting down the rest of the wine, Warren told me they had bought a rental house. Aha, I thought, that's why I'm here. I asked where it was, and he told me. I knew of the house. Was it rented?

"Not right now. It needs some work."

"Something you'd like me to take a look at, maybe?"

"If you have time. I imagine you're pretty busy this time of the year. I thought it might be something you could work on in your odd hours, fit it in around your more important work." He wrinkled his nose and shrugged. "If you're interested."

"I can sure take a look at it." So there it is, I thought. When someone has a little work for you to do on the side, what it really means is they'd like to get the work done cheap. If anyone ever wrote a pamphlet for the shrewd property owner, telling how to get the work done cheap, it might go like this: Get a tradesman who's single. He has more spare time, and he's vulnerable to good grub. When he's working, keep beer in front of him. Pay for the materials yourself when you can, and run the errands. When the job's done, ask him how much you owe him. Pay him on the spot, preferably in greenbacks.

It's all right with me, though. I know how to work that way, too. We agreed to meet at the house at one in the afternoon on Sunday. That's another little rule—in honor of the Sabbath and probable hangovers, don't ever propose to work before noon on Sunday.

* * * * *

The house was a good little fixer-upper, as the realtors say. It was about fifty years old, two bedrooms and a partial base-ment, detached garage, with an evident history of renters and do-it-yourself handymen. I could see at least a month's worth of odd hours and weekends, plus a good way to get rid of odds and ends of materials left over from other jobs.

Everyone likes to save money when they can, and Warren had a good sense of what to do and what not to do. He had kept the electrical service turned on, which made it convenient to have a refrigerator on the job. He already had it there. We drank a couple of beers as we looked over the job and talked about it. We agreed that I would keep track of my own time and materials, I could charge any other materials to his account, and he would help on weekends. Another little rule for the owner: Offer to do the shit work. Corresponding rule for the tradesman: Save it for him.

After the business talk, we had a general beer of friendship, or, as they say on Sundays, fellowship. I asked him if Danny and Renée were on the road by now.

"No, I think they're a little strapped for cash. We might have them as lodgers for a few days."

"Oh. Car repairs knock a hole in their finances?"

"Made things worse. I think they were lodgers in Queer Street before that."

I frowned and cocked my head. "I don't get it."

He smiled, one of those let-me-explain-my-clever-joke smiles. "It's an expression. It means difficulties, especially financial ones."

"Where in the hell did you pick up an expression like that?"

"From Dickens. You know, the British writer."

"Uh-huh. Sounds British," I said. "So you have 'em on your hands for a while?"

"Oh, I don't think it should be that much of a bother. They seem like nice enough kids."

"Seem like it."

The next week was fairly busy for me, so I didn't get to work on Warren's rental until Saturday morning. I decided to start at the beginning, so I took off the old wooden screen and storm door that served as the first entry door onto the front porch. It needed to be tightened, re-squared, and planed down. I left the sanding and painting for Warren, who showed up at mid-morning, a little shaky and in a good humor that seemed forced. He scraped and sanded the door frame while I worked on the main entry door, adjusting the striker plate and nailing down the door stop, then planing the door and varnishing what I planed. We didn't talk much.

At a little before noon he offered to go get some lunch. He came back with hamburgers and a twelve-pack of Budweiser. I could see he imagined this to be a long job, long enough to make it profitable to buy Bud instead of Michelob. That was fine with me, since I usually drink Bud anyway and didn't have to feel shy now about helping myself.

When we were on our second beer, it came out that the lodgers were still with the Ackermans. I asked if it was getting tiresome at all, and he said yes, it was. He grimaced, then added that there were some things he didn't particularly care for.

It seemed like he wanted to talk about it, so I asked, "Anything you can say out loud?"

He tweaked the corners of his mouth and said, "They're helping out."

"Oh."

"Yeah, each day they go out and shoplift something for us."

"Oh, shit."

"Yeah, in a town like this. I told them they didn't have to, and they said they didn't mind."

"What kind of stuff?"

"One day it was T-bones for dinner, another day it was one of those impulse shower heads for the bathroom they're using. Danny installed it for me."

"Real handy, huh?"

"Yeah. I was afraid he'd offer to come over here and help out."

"Then you'd never get rid of 'em."

"You're tellin' me."

We finished our beers, and he fetched us another one. After a respectable pause, he said, "You know how to keep your mouth shut, don't you?"

"Oh, yeah."

"I think he's screwing my wife."

"Oh, shit." I meant it. I didn't like to know that much about the personal life of someone I knew as little as I knew him. It was fine if he wanted to share his beer, but not his dirty laundry. I tried to make light of it by saying, "Too bad you couldn't screw his little girlfriend for him. She's kinda cute. Not that I'd notice."

"Me neither."

We settled into silence for a while, drinking slowly and, it seemed, prolonging the three-beer lunch. Eventually Warren spoke. "That was more or less the reason we invited them to stay."

"Oh?"

"Seemed like they might be fun to play with."

"Oh."

"We invited them home the first night, and nothing happened."

"Uh-huh."

"I think Bev made a little headway in the meanwhile."

"Oh. Uh-huh. Sort of left you out, you think?"

"I think so. Those kids know what's up."

"Just working the job their way."

"Yeah. I think I'll have to give them some travel money to get rid of them." He got up to bring us another beer.

By now I was feeling relaxed and not really anxious to go back to work. On the other hand, I was afraid Warren was going to turn our lunch hour into a further episode of Our Dark Secrets. I was surprised when he didn't. We drank that fourth beer while he told me about the bass fishing this time of the year in Missouri. Then we went back to work.

On Sunday afternoon, he showed up with another twelve-pack, which was good, since we'd finished off the other one before we went home on Saturday. He was in better spirits than the day before, so I figured he either got a hold of Renée or got rid of both of them. We spent a couple of hours scraping and wire-brushing the living room walls, to prep them for painting. It was tedious work, but it had to be done, along with patching cracks in the plaster.

During the 3:00 o'clock beer break, Warren gave an update on his lodgers. "I gave them a hundred dollars to get to Denver on," he said. "I told them they could pay me back when they could afford it."

"Safe bet."

"Yeah, for a mere hundred dollars I'll probably never have to put up with them again."

* * * * *

Things sailed along pretty well for the next month. I worked on the Ackermans' rental from time to time, and a couple of evenings I had dinner with them. Then, one Sunday afternoon, Warren had the troubled look again. We took a break from re-tiling the tub enclosure, and he brought out the subject with the first beer.

"I think there's some trouble brewing at my house."

"Those kids aren't back in town, are they?"

"Oh, no. It's a little different."

"Yeah . . ."

"She's messing around on me."

"Oh. Someone you know?"

"Someone she knows. Arnie Forsberg."

"The tractor salesman?"

"The tractor salesman."

"How would she get tied up with him?"

"He banks where she works."

"Oh. That doesn't sound good."

"It's not."

I thought this might turn into a long beer break, and it did. Eventually it came out that the Ackermans had always liked to play around, sometimes with another couple, sometimes with a single, but always with the understanding that both of them were in on it or at least knew about it. But now, Bev was acting on her own. "You know," he said, "I used to find it exciting that someone was putting the blocks to her, maybe in the next room. Now, it just scares me."

No fun in that, I thought. "Well," I said, "you didn't have anything to do with this one, uh?"

"No, not at all. This sounds like a twisted thing to say, but it's like she's violated our trust."

"I can see that."

"I don't like him at all."

"I've never cared all that much for him."

"I can understand a guy wanting to put a little mud on his turtle, but I wish to hell he'd leave my wife alone."

"Anything you can do about it?"

"Oh, I've raised plenty of hell, but she's more or less let me know she's going to do as she damn well pleases."

"That sucks."

"It makes life very anxious for Warren Ackerman," he said.

We each fell into our own thoughts for a while, and he said, "One time I was in a bar in Missouri, and this guy and his wife were having a drunk-ass argument. Finally the guy says, 'You're just damn lucky I never killed you.' That must have impressed me. The next time my wife and I got into a drunken argument, I tried that line out on her."

"What did Bev say to that?"

"Oh, it wasn't Bev. That was my first wife. When I lived in Missouri."

"I didn't realize you'd been married before."

"Oh, yeah. This is my second and Bev's third. That's what's got me scared. I'm afraid it's going to happen again."

"The 'D' word."

"Yep."

"How long have you and Bev been together?"

"Just six happy years," he said, not without a tinge of sarcasm.

"Anyway, what did the first wife say?"

"She said I was the one who was lucky, for not having the nerve to try. She left me not too long after that. Things were on the rocks by then anyway."

"Nah," I said, "I don't imagine brave talk does all that much good. Not if they want to leave."

"Only one sure way I've heard of to keep a woman."

I sensed that a joke was coming, so I played along. "Oh?"

"I read it in a book. A guy had a dream that the devil came to him and told him that as long as he wore this ring on his finger, his wife would never be untrue to him."

"Really?"

"And then he woke up and found his finger stuck in his wife's ass."

I laughed and spluttered my beer. Warren laughed. I think we'd both been looking for something to laugh at. "Where did you come across that story?"

"It was an old book, maybe four hundred years old. It was a book of jests and merry tales, back in the time of Shakespeare."

"British."

"Yeah."

"Sounds British."

"It's a story you remember."

"I guess so. Does it work?"

"Never tried it. You'd have to take the ring off sooner or later."

We laughed again, and Warren got us another beer. As we drank that one and he told me about the bass fishing in northern California, I had two separate realizations that played back and forth on me. One was that I would never have guessed that Warren and Beverly had been married to anyone but themselves. The other was that during the first year I knew them and used to sit down and have a drink with them, they might have been looking me over as someone to take home. If they did, I'm glad they passed me over. It was better just being their handyman.

* * * * *

In the middle of the next week, when I saw that Warren had gotten telephone service hooked up in the rental, I began to feel sorry for him. It looked like she was giving him the shove, and it's always sad when one party wants the separation and the other doesn't. I was also getting concerned for myself. Petty little accounts like mine are the easiest to hang out to dry when the hammer comes down. Every tradesman I know would agree with me: If you see a divorce or bankruptcy coming, try to get out with what you can.

By now we had the two bedrooms, the bathroom, and the living room all touched up, so it wasn't inconvenient for him to move in. Maybe it would get the work finished sooner, I thought. I also knew he would be around all of the time, and it occurred to me that I didn't know of any real friends of the Ackermans. I was the one guy he could talk to.

When I showed up at the job on Saturday morning, he was living there. The kitchen was pretty well in the torn-up stage, so he had a makeshift table, a cardboard box, set up in the living room. He had a drip coffee maker with a fresh pot of coffee, plus a bag of donuts. He still had the energy to make fun of circumstances, and that helped.

"It looks like I'll be staying here for a while," he said. "I think they call it a 'trial separation' in the trade."

"I've heard it put that way."

"Would you care to join me for a continental breakfast?"

"I would be delighted. Let me get my coffee cup."

He had set up two milk crates to sit on. As he poured my coffee, his hand shook. He looked at me as if to say, yes, it was noticeable.

"Rough night?" I asked.

"Not fun."

"Do we want to go ahead with the kitchen today?"

"Oh, hell, yes. We can't let this other stuff get in the way."

"O.K."

We each ate a donut, and he poured more coffee. "Phone works."

"Is that right?"

"Yeah. I called her last night, not two hours after I left there. She said she was alone, but I heard a toilet flushing in the background."

I made a painful face.

"I have a hard time dealing with that sort of thing," he said. "Why can't people be more discreet?"

"I don't know."

"I remember when I first started going out with Bev. I stayed over at her place one night, and I walked her out to her car in the morning. It was just starting to drizzle rain, and there was a note on her windshield. She opened it, and there was this smeared little message that said, 'I will always love you, Bev.' She just said 'Shit' and crumpled it up and tossed it in the gutter. I felt sorry for the guy, even though I was glad he was out of the picture."

"I can imagine."

"But at least I hadn't parked my car in front of her place."

"You knew the guy was still around."

"It doesn't take that much effort to be discreet."

"No, it doesn't."

"So I told her, when I heard the toilet flush, that I was going to drive by at midnight, and if he was still there, I was going to raise some hell."

"Did you?"

"I did something I wished I hadn't. I sat in the bushes along the front walk there."

"Uh-huh."

"Along about twenty to twelve, old hot shot comes out the front door and closes it behind him, and walks right by me. As soon as he gets past me, he cuts a big fart, just cool as can be, jingles his keys, cranks up his car, and drives off. I could have killed him."

"You didn't go see her then, did you?"

"No, I went slinking out of there. Before I got mad on the phone, I had told her I'd stay away for a week, since she wanted some 'time to herself.' I shouldn't have gone up there."

"Probably not."

"But I was discreet."

"You have that in your favor."

"So was the guy who left the note on her windshield that time."

"I guess he was."

"I think I know how he felt."

"I suppose you do."

* * * * *

It was my seventh weekend on the job, plus a few scattered afternoons and evenings, and some stray materials. I figured Warren was into me for about a thousand dollars, which isn't a real lot unless you get stiffed for it.

The house was empty when I went to work on Sunday afternoon. I was trying to make short work of the basement rooms so I could wrap up the job and get out. I heard Warren come in, and pretty soon he came downstairs. He had taken Bev to Sunday brunch and had had a talk, he said. He had some prospects in Arizona. Real estate was moving a lot better there. Bev would hang around here until she got the two houses sold, and then she would join him there.

I nodded. I would believe it for his sake, even if it sounded like whistling in the dark.

"I wish I could pay you right now," he said, "but I don't have it. I have to borrow from her to leave town."

"I understand."

"I'll make sure Bev pays you when she sells. It's got to be over a thousand by now, isn't it?"

"I'd settle for an even thousand."

"If she pisses up a rope for some reason and doesn't pay you, I'll send it to you."

I nodded.

He glanced around the room we were in. "You just about have it done, haven't you?"

"There's a few more things I'd like to do, like re-hang that flaky closet rod and putty in some nail holes."

He wrinkled his nose. "Hell with it. I'll give it a coat of paint and call it good."

I looked at my watch and then at him. I wondered if it was supposed to go easier on his conscience if he didn't let me finish the job. That way, not paying me wouldn't seem so wrong. But, I thought, we'd already put a price on it. Then I saw what it was. Nothing was funny anymore. He was trying to keep his pecker up in a way that didn't fit him very well, and it pained him to have me see him putting on the front. That's what it was. I nodded slowly. I didn't enjoy seeing him that way, anyway.

"Seriously," he said, turning his mouth down. "Don't worry about this room. I'll finish it up myself." He looked around the room and then at me, as if to say, no, I can't stiff you all the way, not this way. "Shit," he said, pulling out his wallet, "I can at least give you something." He looked into the billfold and hesitated, then pulled out five twenties and handed them to me. "I wish I had more."

"Thanks," I said. "I appreciate it."

He put out his hand, and we shook. "Thanks a lot for every-thing, Mike." He took a deep breath. "You've been a good friend to me, at a time when it mattered. I'll make sure you don't get screwed out of the rest of your wages."

I wondered if his idea of a friend was someone who didn't have to be paid in full. "I trust you," I said, and in a small way, for a moment, I did. A hundred bucks can do that. Besides, there was nothing to be gained if I didn't.

I walked out of that basement room, for the most part feel-ing relieved to be done with the Ackermans. I didn't expect to see the rest of the money, and it's a good thing I didn't count on it. Bev sold the houses a couple of months later, sold them both cheap, I understand, and left right after that. As I heard it, there were a few others around town who would also have liked to see her get better prices for the property.

She didn't leave town with Arnie Forsberg. He's still here, selling tractors and jingling his keys, I guess. I heard she went to Arizona, where she and Warren were going to give it another try. It didn't seem very likely to me, based on what I had seen, but that was their business. Maybe they needed each other.

I didn't have any hopes one way or another for their life together, and I didn't nourish any hopes that they would bounce back financially and remember me. I was just glad to be clear of them. Also, vaguely and at a distance, I cringed for them. Separately or together, they were bound to end up in difficulties. In his way, Warren probably meant it about my being a friend. People who were that nice, like the Ackermans were, just didn't have much in the way of friends. And people who were that nice would always need them.

Orin's Saddle

The last wild geese of winter were gone, and spring was making its slow return. The pale grasses of winter were giving way to green, the sun was becoming warmer as it moved north, and the meadowlarks, or most of them, had returned. Evan had seen the first baby cottontails of the year— two of them sitting at the mouth of their burrow by the woodpile—and was brushing thatches of winter hair out of his horse's coat when he got the call from Travis.

The boy wanted to come by and pick up his father's saddle. Evan said it would be fine, and he agreed to be at home that Saturday, the day before Easter. As he went back to brushing Cisco, he felt the rays of the sun along with the radiant warmth of the horse. This was the time of the year when the world seemed to stir, and he imagined something was going on with Travis as well.

That evening, Evan burned a pile of brush he had cleaned up from the windbreak. April was a good time to burn. What was probably the last snow of the season had just melted, and the new grass was pushing through, so fire danger wasn't very high. Evan brought out a folding chair and sat at the fireside as the branches burned to coals. Thought settled upon him, as if it took thought to watch a fire burn down. He flipped in the unburned ends with his pitchfork, then sat back in his chair. The fire was warm. He could feel it in the brim of his felt hat, in the corduroy collar of his denim jacket. The skin on his face felt smooth and tight. It was a good fire, burning clean.

Something in Travis' voice had said more than the words themselves. All the kid had said was that he would like to come and get the saddle and that it would be good to see Uncle Evan again and talk with him. What he hadn't said, but what Evan had sensed in the boy's half-halting words, was that he had some questions. Evan hadn't seen the kid in a couple of years, and they really didn't have much to talk about, so if Travis had anything on his mind, it probably had to do with his father.

Evan poked at the coals. In some ways it was like a different life to think back on, those days when he and his brother came and went, saw each other every few days, and never thought about when the next time would be.

Life had been easy and open then. They both worked for wages, and the wages were theirs to spend. If they wanted to drive to Cheyenne and dance till the bars closed, they could, and if they wanted to hook up the horse trailer and go to the mountains, they could do that, too. Evan felt an ache in his throat as some of the old feeling came back—and it was not just the old feeling but a mix of what had been and what was no more.

Evan remembered the cold country the best, when they would sleep in the camper on the back of the pickup, leave camp in the cold darkness, and be on a ridge top when the sun came up. He could remember looking down and seeing their camp, with the pickup and horse trailer and rope corral, and the horses waiting in case there would be meat to pack out. It had always been a glorious feeling to be on top of the big country at sunrise, knowing his brother was on another ridge taking it all in on his own, the two of them separately waiting for the magic of elk in the timber.

There had been other trips, countless ones, when they had summer-camped around a fire like this one, or later in the year when they had gone out for deer and antelope. Once in October they had gone all the way to the Powder River country up by Kaycee, to the ranch of some folks Orin had met. The people raised sheep, and they had a low, snug barn where Evan and Orin had rolled out their beds the first night, fixed breakfast in the morning, and hung and skinned their two deer by noon. Evan always remembered that barn, with the soft straw they had slept in. He also remembered the deer, both of them three-pointers, which had come up the draw together right at sunrise.

Orin had always liked to take his pickup on those trips because he liked to drive. He didn't care to cook or do dishes, but he always did his share around camp, whether they were just camping or hunting as well. When they killed game, the two brothers worked together at the dragging, loading, or hoisting, and they took turns at the skinning. One always knew what the other was doing, and the two-man jobs went smoothly without much necessary talk. If one of them took the first hold, the other knew where to grab. That was the way it had been.

Evan smiled. It was like loading firewood. Sometimes in the fall, in between hunting and before the big snows, they would go out to the hills and cut a load of firewood. When it looked like they had enough cut, one of them would climb into the pickup bed while the other stayed on the ground. Then it was a game to keep the pieces coming, so that the guy stacking set a rhythm and picked the pieces out of the air. The guy on the ground, wherever he was, tried to pitch every piece so that it hung in the air right where the other man would turn to grab it.

When half of a team was gone, there was a lot missing. There had come a time, even when Orin was still alive, that the two of them no longer did things together. Even then, as Evan looked back on it now, he had assumed things would go back to the way they had been when uncounted chunks of firewood hung in mid-air.

It was after Orin had married Heather, and after Travis was born, that things went bad. And when they went bad with Orin, they went bad between the brothers. At the time it had seemed as if there was no real way to fix things, since it was beyond anything they had between them. Evan had thought it was just a matter of time, waiting for Orin to get through it. Evan assumed that when Orin did get out onto the other side of the bad time, they would go back to doing what they had always done together.

Evan leaned forward and shaped up the pile of glowing coals. He squinted. Who could say why things went bad when they did? Who could say where the blame should go? He had always liked Heather, and when it became known to him that Orin had taken an interest in someone else, he could not find a way to tell his brother how it went against his grain. And when he saw Heather with a strange man at the Diamond Horseshoe, forty miles away, he did not know how to feel. At some level he felt it was Orin's fault, and Orin had never said anything that made it seem otherwise. Looking back, Evan knew he would have stuck up for his brother if Orin had thought he deserved it, but instead, there had been dead air between them.

That had been a bad stretch of time—more than three years, as he counted it off later. Orin and Heather divorced. The other woman went away with her husband. Heather married the other man and moved away, and within a year after that, they had another little boy. Then one day, before things ever got better, Orin hit a patch of ice and slid his pickup into the Sybille Canyon, and Evan came to realize it was too late to fix anything.

Evan had seen it in others, not to mention in himself, that when everything had gone to hell in a fellow's life, he didn't like to answer to anybody. He didn't want to have to explain, no matter how well-meaning the question might be. He wanted to get through it and then talk about it, if at all, when it was in the past. That was the way it had seemed with Orin, as if it was just as well to let his gloom settle on its own. Then the two of them could talk about it, when things had brightened up.

But when another season rolled around, Evan found himself stacking firewood on the tailgate, then climbing up into the pickup and re-stacking the wood in back of the cab. He handled every piece twice, working both sides of the stack, and he turned the same thoughts over and over, with no answers.

Now it seemed as if there might be something to talk about after all. From the sounds of it, Travis wanted to know something, wanted to know about a story that ended before it was over. The kid was old enough to drive, old enough to come visit Uncle Evan by himself. He was old enough to think he wanted his father's saddle, so he was probably old enough to have questions.

* * * * *

On Saturday morning, Evan sat on the back steps in the morning sunshine and drank a cup of coffee. The two little rabbits were out nibbling grass, and the silver tinkle of the meadowlarks fluted on the clear morning air. Evan watched a fly crawl up the trim on the door. He thought it was the first fly he had seen this spring. He smiled. If Uncle Wilson were here, he'd be after it with a whip.

Evan closed his eyes for a long moment in the morning sun, then opened them and took a drink of coffee. Uncle Wilson. Evan remembered the day his father and Uncle Wilson came back from the hospital when Aunt Liz was sick. Uncle Wilson had his head down, so Evan could see only his hat brim as he came up the walkway. Evan's father had his left arm across his brother's shoulders and was looking at him, saying something. Evan remembered how clearly he could tell, just from looking out the window, that Aunt Liz was gone. And that empty feeling always came back when Evan recalled the picture of the two McCabe brothers, Wilson and Cameron, walking from the pickup to the house.

Evan let out a long breath. His father had said Uncle Wilson didn't take to swatting flies until after Aunt Liz died. It was a habit he got into when he lived alone, and he lived that way for another twenty years. Then a couple of years before he died, he took it into his mind that he wanted to see the ocean. He and Aunt Liz had never had any children, and he said he wanted someone to go with him. He told his brother Cam that he'd like one of the boys to drive him.

Orin was just starting to date Heather at that time, and Evan didn't have a steady girlfriend, so he got elected. He drove Uncle Wilson's 1954 Oldsmobile all the way to the coast. It was a heavy old warhorse, twenty years old but in tip-top condition, and Evan opened it up pretty well out on the Nevada desert.

When they dropped down into California, Uncle Wilson said he didn't want to see the ocean in no damn city, so Evan studied the map and took a series of two-lane highways around to the north of San Francisco. He finally brought the Oldsmobile to a stop at a place called Point Reyes. He thought they must be quite a picture in the dark green Oldsmobile with its sun visor and bucking bronco plates—a pale old cowboy in a grey hat and dark glasses, chauffeured by a young cowboy in a white straw hat and sideburns.

Evan wondered how long the old man would want to sit and watch the ocean, but before the nephew had a chance to get out of the car and smell the sea breeze, he heard his uncle say, "So that's it." Evan turned and saw the old man nod and then twist his mouth. Still looking forward, he said, "I don't see that much foo-fo-raw about it. But we seen it." He looked at Evan and said, "I suppose we can go back now." Evan gunned up the old Oldsmobile and dropped it into reverse, and as he backed out he caught a glimpse of his uncle sitting with his hands in his lap. He could tell the old man was satisfied.

* * * * *

At a little after ten in the morning, Evan saw a blue-grey car coming down the lane. It was a mid-sized car with a round nose and wrap-around taillights, just like all the cars that were out these days, but it was obviously a kid's car. It had a black stripe across the bottom of the door and side panel, and it had tinted windows with a "No Fear" sticker in the window behind the driver's seat.

As Travis got out of the car, Evan could tell it was Orin's son. He was nearly as tall as his father and had the same build—square shoulders, blocky hips. His hair was lighter than Orin's, almost a dishwater blond, and he had it hacked the way boys his age wore it these days. As he came closer, Evan saw the golden glint of a loop earring in the boy's left ear lobe. Evan told himself that was getting to be normal these days, too. It was still the same kid.

After they had shaken hands and exchanged greetings, Evan invited Travis inside, where they sat at the kitchen table at right angles and sipped coffee. They went through the small talk about Travis' family, the road conditions, and the weather. Then there was a lull, and Evan figured he could just let it be or he could give the kid a chance. The second way would be harder, but he took it.

"Was there anything in particular that you wanted to talk about while you were here?"

Travis stared at his coffee cup, which he was holding with both hands on the table in front of him. The left side of his face winced, and he said, "There was somethin'."

"Uh-huh." Evan waited, and the nephew just sat there, still staring at his cup. After a moment Evan said, "Well, we could give it a try."

"It's about my dad."

"Thought it might be."

Travis sipped his coffee and set the mug back down, still between his hands. "It doesn't seem like something I can ask at home." He looked up.

Evan nodded. He had met the step-father, Downing, and he could imagine the family of three Downings and a McCabe. "I think I can understand that."

Travis bit his lower lip, then asked, "Do you know why my mom and my dad split up?"

Evan shook his head. "I sure don't. Your dad and I were pretty close, of course, but I never got a story on that." He paused. It seemed the kid deserved more, so he went on. "Sometimes a couple starts out together, and everything goes fine, and then something between 'em changes. Sometimes it's something that one of 'em does, and sometimes things just go wrong between 'em. Then they might go on and do things that just make things worse." A memory flashed of Heather and the other man, before Evan knew him as Downing. Evan shook his head. "I don't know which way it was with your folks. When things went bad, I wasn't talking' with 'em very much. And after that—well, it was too late."

Travis gave a slight nod. He had his eyes fixed on his cup again.

Evan could tell the kid wasn't satisfied. There must be more to the question, he thought, so he said, "I guess it's something you've been wonderin' about."

Travis scratched the underside of his ear with his thumb, and the earring moved. He winced and said, "There's this kid I know in Douglas. I mean, he's not a good friend, but we know each other."

"O.K.."

"Well, he's got a cousin that lives here."

Evan did a quick mental check and didn't come up with an answer. Then he figured it didn't matter—at this point, anyway. Travis was still hesitating, so he said, "And the kid over here passed on something to the kid you know."

Travis's eyes went down and came back up to his uncle. "Yeah." He swallowed, then spoke. "He said my dad had an affair with a married woman, and her husband had to take her away."

Evan felt the anger flare inside him. Maybe Orin deserved to have it said that way, but the kid didn't. "I'll tell you," he said, taking a breath and making himself be careful, "it's a chickenshit thing to do, to bad-mouth a kid's father to him, especially when the father isn't around anymore. These kids don't know any better, and whoever they got it from probably doesn't, either." Evan shook his head. "I'd be better off not knowin' who it is." He licked his lips. "But I'll tell you, he was your father." Evan felt his eyes watering, but he pushed himself on. "Whatever he did or didn't do, he was your father. And no trashy talk can change that. He was a good man, and you've got a right to be proud of him."

Evan wiped his eyes and sniffled, which must have been a cue for the kid to do the same.

Travis looked up, his face red and his blue eyes watery. "But did he do it?"

"You mean, have the affair?" Evan's throat was tight.

Travis nodded. "Yeah."

Evan moistened his lips and raised his eyebrows, hesitating. He had always thought Orin was wrong in what he had done, but Orin was his brother, and at gut level, Evan had always known he should stick up for him. Now he had the choice of not speaking well of a boy's father or not telling the truth to his brother's son. He wanted to put the blame back on whoever had started the talk, but it was too late for that. The kid was waiting for an answer, had been waiting for several long seconds. Evan tried to imagine what Orin had been thinking about all of it back then, whether he was sorry he had any part of it. Then he wondered, in less than a second more, what Orin would have said to his own son. The answer was not so hard then. Evan said, "I think it's possible he might have done something like that."

The kid nodded and tucked his lips in against his teeth.

The uncle went on. "Like I said, I don't know what happened first, or how any of it got started, or what order it all happened in. There was a lot more to it than either you or I is ever likely to know, and it's probably better that way." He paused. "But there's some basis to what you heard."

Travis nodded and wiped his eyes again.

Evan felt his own eyes water again as he said, "But he was your father. And he was my brother. No sonofabitch can take that from us."

Travis sniffed. "Yeah, I know. But I just had to ask."

* * * * *

When it came time to load up the saddle, the uncle asked the kid if he wanted anything to go with it, like a pad and blanket, or a bridle.

Travis said he didn't know.

Evan said he could always come back for any of those things if he wanted, or for any other reason.

As the blue-grey car drove away, Evan felt as if part of his brother was in the back seat, but at the same time he felt as if whatever he had had of his brother was still whole. He had done as well as a fellow might. He had had a brother and had done right by him. The kid had a brother, too, so some day he might come to see how it all worked.

Waltz Across Utah

She stepped back into my life in the lower level of the lounge car. On the way out to the coast I had gotten into a siege of poker, which ended when the train took on a load of worn-out gamblers in Reno—people who packed the car and then nursed drinks all the way back to suburbia, people who made even a two-bit-limit game of dealer's choice seem tawdry. Now, on the return trip, as the train crawled up the grade from the valley, the lower level had an assortment of backgammon players, cribbage duelists, and casual drinkers like myself, all of whom, voluntarily or less so, were hearing the varied offerings of Tom.

Tom was a latter-day country-rock-folk singer. He was not paid by Amtrak; he was just a passenger, bound for Omaha, who was happy to strum his guitar, sip beer, and meet people. He was the type of performer who welcomed requests and tried to honor them, even if it meant doing only part of the song, borrowing chords, asking for lyrics, or getting others to help sing. His main strength as a performer was not a vast repertory of well-practiced songs, but his flair for bringing people together and getting them to have fun.

It worked with me, for one. He learned early that I was willing to request songs, that I knew some of the words to many songs, that his first name and my last name were the same, that together we could piece together "Hang Down Your Head, Tom Dooley," that I was from Wyoming, that I would buy him a

Miller Lite while I got a Budweiser for myself, that I did not play the guitar but sang inoffensively.

The long, unhurried pull up from the valley through Donner Pass is speechlessly beautiful, especially in winter, with the snow and the evergreens and the blue sky and the bluer blue of Donner Lake and the curtains of icicles on the rock shelves just outside the starboard window. When the *ooh's* and *ah's* sounded, Tom laid off the guitar until the scenery became more routine. Then he would drop back a verse, or warm up with the refrain, or pick up where he left off.

We worked our way through train songs like "The Rock Island Line" and "The Wabash Cannonball," the inevitable "Me 'n' Bobby McGee," standards like "Walkin' the Floor Over You" (in itself a trick sometimes, on the rolling deck), and "Your Cheatin' Heart." Somebody said that Merle Haggard was playing at Tahoe, and Tom took up a couple of Merle's songs—"Mama Tried," which got a great chorus from the passengers, and "Big City," where he dropped in "Wyoming" in place of "Montana" in the refrain.

The group ran out of requests then, as if we had hit a lull. Tom looked at me.

"What would you like to hear, Ken?"

"Hell, I don't know. I like 'em all." I looked at the other people, many of them on their way to Reno, and I thought of an old Woody Guthrie song. "Do you know 'Philadelphia Lawyer'?" I asked.

"Do you know there's a woman dyin' upstairs?"

"What?" I asked back.

"No, but if you hum a couple of bars I can fake it."

"Oh."

"Sorry. Just workin' my night club act. Seriously, though, 'Philadelphia Lawyer'?"

"Yeah. Woody Guthrie song."

"Oh . . . yeahhh." He studied his hat brim as he plunked out the chords. "Yeah. I've got the melody. You might have to feed me a few lines. It starts out like this, doesn't it?—

> *Way-yout in Ree-no Nevadder*
> *Where romances bloom and then fade,*
> *A great Philadelphia lawyer*
> *Was in love with a Hollywood maid.*

He really laid on the twang as he worked his way through the stanzas about Wild Bill the gun-totin' cowboy, and how Wild Bill, seeing the silhouettes of the shifty lawyer and Bill's sweet-heart on her window shade, heard the shyster say,

> *"Come, love, and we will wander*
> *Out where the lights are so bright..."*

By now, six verses or so into the song, he had gained enough control over it that he could improvise. Instead of having the lawyer try to seduce her to leave the cowboy and go to Philadelphia, he tossed in

> *"Come go with me to Wy-o-ming*
> *And leave these damn gamblers behind."*

Then he finished off with the last stanza as it was, and he collected a patter of applause.

By this time the seats had filled up, and I had lost mine the last time I had gone for beer. So I had been standing, slightly flexed at the knees, swaying to the rock of the train and the beat of "Philadelphia Lawyer," and enjoying the feeling that I didn't have a thing to think about for another twenty-six hours, when I would get off the train in Denver. Time was something we moved through, like the landscape, and both would come together—Denver, and whenever we got there.

I tossed my beer can into the tall, rigid, paper trash bag, then turned to walk to the snack stand. As I did so, I lurched to the left with the sway of the train, straightened up, and came face to face with a woman who had stepped out from the staircase. A chill surged through my forehead and down through my arms, and my heart and stomach felt a jolt.

"Well, hello," I said, so sure that I didn't have to ask. "You're Peggy."

"My God," she said, apparently just as shocked. "You're Ken Thomas, aren't you?"

"Yeah." A forced laugh. "I sure am . . . I was just going for drinks. For Tom there, and me. Can I get you something? A drink?" I looked at her. "Are you with someone?"

"No, I'm by myself."

"Well—a drink, then?"

"To tell the truth, I was on my way to the restroom. After that, I'm sure I could drink something. They have mixed drinks, don't they?"

"Sure."

"No, wait. I'd rather have one of those cute little bottles of white wine. Could you get me one?"

"Sure," I said, happy to have a moment of recovery.

She turned away, then stopped and looked back, and shook her head. "I can't believe I bumped into you."

"I'm pretty surprised, too," I admitted.

Once I'd delivered Tom's beer and made sign language that I had other business to tend to, I joined Peggy and followed her up the narrow stairwell to the observation level. There were no seats empty. "Well," I said. "There weren't really any seats down below, either. What do you think?"

"The dining car? It should be after lunch and before dinner."

"I'll see what I can do." More accurately, I went to see what five dollars would do, along with a few words to the steward. He said we could sit there until the first call for dinner, which would be in about an hour.

By the time we were seated at our table, the shock seemed to have worn off in both of us. Peggy sat across the table from me as she had years ago—elbows on the table, hands touching, thumbs against her chin. She wrinkled her nose as she studied me. "It's been nearly twenty years. So much has gone on, and yet it seems so short, you know? Where do we start?" She shrugged, wincing just a little. I saw little crows' feet at the corners of her eyes, light wrinkles on her forehead.

"Well," I said, "we could start with the present. Where are you going?"

"Reno."

"Coming from . . . ?"

"Oakland. East Bay, anyway."

"By yourself."

"Yes."

"Live there? Visiting? Reno, that is."

"Visiting, I guess you could say. And you?"

"Going to Denver, coming from Sacramento— Modesto, actually, but I got on in Sacramento."

"And what takes you to Denver?"

"I live north of there, in Wyoming."

"Wyoming," she said, drawing her brows together. "That *would* be north of Denver, wouldn't it? Do you have a . . . family there?"

"Kind of."

"I didn't mean to—"

"No, that's O.K. You see, I *was* married, but my wife . . . passed on. Not too long ago, less than two years. I have two stepkids—a son and a daughter. Great kids." I sipped my beer.

"What kind of work do you do in Wyoming? Isn't there a lot of coal there?"

"There is, but not where I am. I work in the county assessor's office. Your turn. What do you do?"

"Well, I teach part time at two different schools in the East Bay."

"High schools?"

"Both two-year colleges. I teach composition and creative writing."

"Then you must be on a break now."

"That's right."

I picked my words with care. "I wouldn't expect you had become much of a gambler."

"No," she said, "I haven't. I'm going there to visit a . . . a fellow I know. He plays in one of the smaller clubs there."

"Do you still play? Your guitar?"

"Sometimes."

A silence hung between us as we sat in the empty dining car, hearing the soft clackety-clack.

"It's a pretty trip," she said. "Were you visiting your family in Modesto? Your parents?"

"Yeah. I hadn't been back for Christmas in a while, and both my parents are retired now, so I thought I ought to."

We had a lot to cover, all about what we had done since those days when I was an inquisitive farm boy tired of milking cows, and she was a bohemian refugee from the middle class, concerned with world hunger and social change. It came out that I was still a country boy, living on a little acreage. I learned that she had kept the faith and still avoided the materialism we had both sworn off so long ago. Tired of protesting the war, she had joined the Peace Corps and gone to Ecuador. That was after I, also tired of protesting, had gone on to a tour of duty as a typist in Fort Benning, Georgia. That's how we had gotten separated, although we didn't mention it now. Since I hadn't resisted the draft, I hadn't thought she'd care to stay in touch, so I had let things fade.

Gradually, as we sketched in our pasts, we came back around to the present. She didn't say much about her personal life; she pieced together an income with part-time teaching appointments, had published a few poems in modest magazines, and had become a habitual jogger. For my part I told how I had been married for twelve years to a woman named Marilyn, whose children were now old enough to live on their own.

"What did she die of?"

"A brain hemorrhage. Not a bit of a warning, not even a headache that I knew of. Just here one day, and gone."

"And the kids are on their own?"

"They got a tidy little settlement from her and from their father. That will at least get them through college."

"What became of their father?"

"He was in the war when you and I were in college together. Not to put too fine a point on it, I lived with his military photograph."

"Oh."

We listened to the muffled clackety-clack for a short while.

"And you, Peggy? Have you ever been married?"

"Once. For a couple of years. But the guy changed on me."

"You mean he turned . . . uh . . . gay?"

"Oh, no. He became obsessed with income and consumer toys."

"What did he do?"

"He was a harmless graduate student in history, until he got the fever. Then he talked his parents into putting him through law school. I stuck it out as long as I could."

"No kids?"

"Oh, no."

"What name do you go by?"

"Oh, I still go by Chandler."

"This was after Ecuador?"

"Yes. After I came back and went to work on my master's."

I got her to talk about Ecuador, which was more interesting, and that took us to the steward's first call for dinner. As people moved to the diner, we found a couple of seats in the observation car. I went for drinks, gave the high sign to Tom, and returned to sit with Peggy. We were faced right into the mountainside.

"You're going all the way through to Denver, uh?"

"That's the plan."

"We'll be in Reno in another hour," she said, with a tone of uncertainty.

"Well," I said, sort of like testing the ice before taking a step out onto a pond, "maybe we could trade addresses. Keep in touch, and not wait another twenty years."

"Too bad you can't stay over in Reno a day." Her voice was stone cold and rock steady.

I was starting to feel dizzy, like things had gone unreal and dreamy. "I might be able to," I heard myself say. "How about your friend?"

"He doesn't get off work till midnight."

I took a deep breath. "I don't know. Maybe I can change my ticket and find a room."

"I don't mean to be leading you on," she said, looking straight at me.

"No, I understand. I'd like to be able to. Just visit a while longer." I took a drink of my beer. "But I don't want to interfere with whatever you have with your friend."

"I wouldn't be dragging you into anything," she said.

"Well . . ."

"Seriously, I'd just like to visit with you some more. You won't be endangering anything." She was staring at the rock outside.

"No?" At that moment, my gaze was caught by a small clear stream splashing down a crevice in the rock and spilling over a festoon of icicles. I was taken by the beauty and the simplicity of it, happening all by itself in the middle of the mountains.

With my attention arrested by the stream and the icicles, I heard her say, "No, because I'm not that stuck on him. Sometimes things are good with him, and sometimes I have half a mind to tell him to flake off. You know what I mean."

* * * * *

Matters in Reno were hectic at first. The train stops in the middle of town, so it doesn't wait long. I rushed to the ticket window, changed my travel schedule, dashed back on board to yank my overnight bag, pulled my suitcase from the luggage rack down in the landing of my car, and waved to Tom through the lounge car window. He gave me thumbs up.

Peggy recommended that I stay at the Riverside, one of the less exorbitant hotels, where she said she'd meet me at 9:00. Then she was gone, before the dust had quite settled. I had two and a half hours. Feeling keyed up, I walked the half-dozen blocks in no time, checked into one of the discount package rooms, called my stepson Brad to meet me a day later, waited for the hot water (long way from the boiler), and showered. Even after I had read the brochure on the history of my hotel, I had nearly two hours to kill.

Reno is an entertaining place, as the weekend and holiday hordes can testify, but if a person isn't there to drink and gamble, it's easy to miss the charm of all the glitter and the stale cigarette smoke. I wandered around the Riverside casino, nursing a beer, playing a few slot machines, and trying to keep from feeling desolate. I returned to the bar to redeem my other free drink coupon. There I played a few slow games of Keno, recalling the afternoon's moments as I watched the numbers light up on the board.

Other memories came pouring in as I sat there idle, in a place that would otherwise be depressing. I thought of a distant time and a better place, Peggy's garage apartment, where I first learned to eat yogurt, grind coffee, drink wine, and stay in bed rather than go to class. She had a roommate who, I believe, missed class elsewhere in similar fashion, so that my memories of Peggy's place were usually of the evening and morning. In the evening the place smelled of incense, sometimes blended with wine or coffee; my memory of an evening has her sitting in a muted light, on a large cushion, playing and singing the song "Suzanne" so much like Judy Collins that she seemed not to be Peggy. My morning memory is of the sun rising, as in the Donne poem she liked so much, and shining through the hand-dyed curtains.

There were times when we were apart, times when I returned to my rented room to study history or economics or accounting, happy knowing that I was not a model student and for good reason. There were also evenings I spent alone, drinking supermarket beer and listening to the coarser music that throbbed on my little stereo. On my solitary mornings I would eat cold cereal, drink a cup of instant coffee, and listen to Bob Dylan's very first album, where he did a raucous and exuberant version of an old ballad called "Pretty Peggy-O." Now, as I sat at the bar of a filmy hotel casino, I realized I had lost that album somewhere along the way.

"You won."

"What?" I asked. I blinked my eyes and saw the Keno girl.

"You won. Seventeen and a half dollars."

"Well," I said, as she was paying me off, "I'll have to come in here more often." I wasn't really thinking, just making small talk, because my mind was on Peggy. I let my eyes rest for a couple of seconds on the Keno girl's half-exposed bosom.

She tolerated my gaze, perhaps correlated it with my small talk, and then, still all politeness and business, asked, "Play again?"

"Sure," I said, feeling guilty for being caught looking, and tacky for being in a place where it didn't matter. When she left, I piddled the money away, back to the Keno coffers.

Peggy showed up about ten minutes earlier than we'd arranged, and we went to the restaurant for dinner. I had the seafood platter and she had chicken, so we ordered a liter of white wine and settled into conversation. For the first part of the evening, she seemed more interested in listening than in divulging much about herself. My vocational life wasn't much to talk about, but my domestic life seemed to interest her.

"What did your wife, Marilyn, do for a living?"

"She mainly housewifed—took care of the kids, kept the house, that sort of thing. And she was usually active in some community service or another."

"So yours was a conventional breadwinner-and-housewife arrangement?"

"Not exactly. I didn't really support them. She had a pretty fair nest egg when I met her, and her family invested it for her, so she was comfortable and self-supporting. We were careful to keep her money in her name and in trust for the kids."

"I see. So you wouldn't be thought to be living off of her, or her off of you."

"Exactly. That's why I kept a job. I didn't really need it. I could have been the clever investor and ace entrepreneur, but I felt a lot better keeping out of it. And the neighbors respected me for having a job."

"You lived in town, then."

"Yes, at her place. It had been paid off by insurance. For tax purposes, and to have a little retreat, we bought the place where I live now. I still make payments on it."

"And the house in town?"

"Brad lives in it for right now. We plan to sell it to cover some of his and Kerry's college expenses."

"You stay close with them, then?"

"Oh, yeah. We get along swell, just like always."

"But you live on your own."

"I don't think I ever planned it that way, but that's the way it turned out. After she was gone, I took to staying there for longer and longer stretches, until I finally moved in for good. It's a little ten-acre place pretty much off to itself, with an old farmhouse that suits me O.K."

"You've got animals there?"

"Yes. I keep a couple of horses and raise a few beef calves. It's peaceful there, and I don't have to deal with the world very much."

"Sounds like you've done a pretty good job of it all along. Excuse me, that came out sounding more critical than I meant it to."

"No, that's O.K. You're right. I *have* kept out of the main current, sort of like a solitary duck in my little backwater."

"Some of us born to be swan, and some of us born to be duck."

"What's that?" I asked, perking up at an apparent rendition of someone else's voice.

"That was a saying I picked up from a girl I knew in college the second time around. She had been a refugee from Cambodia, well-to-do over there, but just happy to be getting by over here."

"Hmmm. Sort of a cute saying. And you, Peggy? Do you see yourself as a swan or a duck?"

"She thought I was a swan, because I could play music, and sing, and write poetry. I guess there is some of that in me, but I see myself as more of a duck—as far as my lacklustre line of work goes, anyway. But tell me more about your little retreat, as you called it. Do you have a garden?"

"Oh, yeah. Still a farmer. I raise a vegetable garden every spring and summer—shorter season than I grew up with, but I do O.K. I've also taken more of a fancy to growing flowers."

"And you raise your own meat, cowboy-like?"

"I raise more than I eat, and I eat other things as well. I hunt a little bit, and I shop at the store just like other people do. I'm not your classic recluse mountain man, hidden off in my cabin full of empty whiskey bottles and buffalo hides, with tobacco juice dripping from my beard."

"Well, it sounds pleasant."

"It really is." I toyed with a scallop for a couple of seconds, then took my brave little leap. "You ought to think about coming to see it sometime, when you get some time off." I ate the scallop and took a sip of wine. When I brought my eyes back to her, she was waiting for me.

"I'll give it some thought," she said.

As we finished our meals and worked our way through the liter of wine (which our waitress called a "litter"), I began to understand why Peggy was reserved about her own circumstances. Her life at present was, as she put it, sort of a stagnant pond.

She had worked diligently on her degree and had committed herself to teaching, then tried to work her way into a profession that was tough to break into. She had started with a part-time job and had gone on to put together two and at one point three part-time appointments, all of which paid less, together, than the same amount of work would pay in a full-time appointment.

"It's a noble calling," she explained, "but the system really stinks. In most places the departments are all tenured up, and often with some fairly un-inspired people taking up those jobs. And when there is an opening, the competition is *really* tough. I've put in my time at this for six years now, waiting for my break, but it doesn't seem as if it's going to happen. I seem to be in a dead-end job that doesn't give much in return."

I wondered, at that moment, whether her personal life might be described in similar terms, but I knew I'd have to wait to learn more about that. "Then that's the duck part," I said. "How about the swan? Do you have any ambitions there?"

"I work along in my own quiet way," she said. "I'd like to bring out a book of poems, some that have been published and some that haven't. And I'd like to be able to devote a little more time to my song writing. My profession is supposed to sponsor those endeavors, but so far, it hasn't done so very generously. Quite to the contrary, it's taken quite a bit out of me."

I began to envision a plan, of Peggy finding the time and the place to do those things, in my little old sod shanty on the plains. I also knew that if I advanced this plan too quickly, I would muff it badly. "Have you thought about trying to write for a living?" I asked.

"I'm pretty sure I couldn't do journalism. And I know I couldn't produce commercial romances. I might be able to do free-lance articles, but that would take a lot to break into, too."

From just that much I germinated a seed of hope, like a bean in my garden. As it began to feel its own life force, the bean would shed its skin, burgeon into a sprout, push off slabs of earth, and send out rich green leaves. Then it was at the mercy of sun, wind, hail, late frost, and pests; it was my job to protect what I had helped to bring to life, so that it might flourish and produce.

As I danced with Peggy that evening, it seemed as if life was beginning all over. I was at a pitch of arousal that was almost, but not quite, erotic. My senses floated; I smelled her hair, I was revisited by the faint smell of her person, I felt her body glide with mine, I felt her kiss my cheek as I kissed hers, and I felt her soft breath in my ear as she whispered, "It's nice to be with you again." All this time I was nurturing my hope, yet telling myself not to let it grow into a fantasy that would shame me to look at it. And so I hoped, and told myself not to hope too wildly, and danced one song after another with her. Once I thought of her man, playing a guitar or keyboard in another club in town, looking at the dancers and thinking of his lady, or maybe someone else's, and then I didn't think of him anymore. For so long as we danced, she was mine. As I closed my eyes and felt her warmth and moisture, I allowed myself the hope that she would take root in my life. Her arms around my neck were like the tendrils of a growing plant—reaching, opening, yearning to bask beneath a glorious sun and sky.

* * * * *

For the most part, I was glad to get out of Reno. It's not a pleasant place to kill time, and I dawdled through the morning, knowing that even if I stayed longer, things were not liable to develop much more. I had to leave; she had to go back the other way. Furthermore, she was with her boyfriend. All I could accomplish now was to keep the possibilities open.

When Peggy met me for lunch, I could tell our present encounter had already hit its peak. I gathered that things had not set well with her boyfriend, whose name I learned was Roger. Other than that, our conversation kept away from major issues. I amused her with a summary of an inspirational program I had seen on television in the room, and she told me about a meditation retreat she had gone on a couple of years before.

It was time to leave. The best I could do was hug her and renew my invitation to come visit.

"There might be a way I could do that," she said. "I'll work on it."

"If there's any little thing I can do—"

"Like take your buckboard to meet me at the station?"

"Something like that."

"I'll work on it."

Then she was gone, and I had three empty hours until the train arrived. I read a couple of magazines at the station, started to write her a letter, and went for a last bitter jousting with the one-armed bandits.

Maybe it was just me and my morose frame of mind, but the train seemed more downbeat than it had the day before. I imagined that yesterday's train had, by now, brought Tom almost to Omaha. I have heard the old proverb that a person never steps in the same river twice—that time and change are always coursing along. So it was with the train; I had stepped off somewhat festive and jittery, and now, twenty-four hours later, I stepped back onto a different train in a different mood.

One nice feature was that a large number of people had stopped off in Reno, and I had a double seat to myself. Chances were pretty good that the train would not fill up again until the next morning at Salt Lake City.

I rather envied some of the women, who, regardless of age, seemed to be engrossed in the various works of one author. I had looked at some of these books in a variety store in Reno, and I had an idea of what they were about. They were a series of prehistoric sagas with female characters who, in a caveman world, were coping with modern dilemmas. I envied the women readers because I did not have a handy method for setting aside my own worries and taking up the improbable but satisfying exploits of others. So I bought a pack of trivia cards in the lounge car and whiled away the evening with trivial details I would never remember or use.

I fell asleep for a while, and when I awoke at around midnight, most of the passengers were sprawled out in their seats asleep. I hoped they were having happy cavewoman dreams.

One glance told me that the lounge car was shut down, so I returned to my own car and went to the lower level. Outside the rest room, I poured myself a cup of cold water from the dispenser and had myself a leisurely drink. It was a clear, cold night out on the desert, and I stood there and watched the sagebrush as the train made its way along. The upper half of the door, the window part, swung inwards, so I opened it and stood by the cold opening for several miles. I couldn't smell anything but the cold—no diesel exhaust, no sagebrush, no railroad creosote. It was a pleasant sensation to be visiting with the cold, stark desert, every mile of which seemed, at first, to be a broader barrier between Peggy and me. Then I thought of it as a link, a long expanse of honest land that reached from her to me, and I felt as friendly toward the desert as I always had. I drank a second and then a third paper cup of water, with a gulp of desert each time for a chaser. The night was assuring, and when I returned to my seat, I was optimistic that I would see her again.

When I met Brad at the station in Denver, he had a smile on his face.

"Sounds to me like you've been having an interesting vacation."

"Better than a night at the laundromat. Actually, it's kind of an interesting story, but not as racy as we might like it to be."

"Glad you had a good time."

"I guess I did," I answered, "but that's an awfully long ride. Saw some pretty country, though—lots of deer, and a few elk."

On the way home, I sketched in the story for Brad.

"Well, hell yes," he said, "I hope she comes out to visit."

"Horses O.K.?"

"Just fine."

"Any excitement for you in the meanwhile?"

"Not much. Shovel snow and sit by the fire."

"Think we might stop in Cheyenne and stimulate their failing economy to the tune of a six-pack or so?"

" 'Magine," he said. He drew out his can of chew, pinched a wad for his lower lip, and turned up George Strait on the tape player. I was happy to be home.

* * * * *

I got back into to my routine of going to work, coming home, and doing my chores. I resumed my habits as wearing long johns and double wool socks around the place. We were still in a pretty good freeze, and I had hay to restack, snow to shovel, ice to try to clear out from walkways, and horses to brush and pick. As I went about those tasks, I began to take a fresh look at my horse barn and tack shed, my gates and corrals, my garden plot, my flower beds, and even my wood pile. In them I saw plans that had become achievements, not always perfect, but improvements on my little parcel here on the vast plains. Dear as it was to me, though, I realized that if Peggy came here, she would not see these things as anything but the usual calendar and postcard features that presumably came with the territory. With time she might see them as more, but I agreed with myself that I would have to risk it.

Another recurring thought I had during this time, or maybe fantasy would be a better word, was the wish that some day I would come home from work and find her at my place. I didn't know what kind of car to hope for—just some modest, unfamiliar sedan—but it didn't matter because there was never another car there.

About a month after I returned, in early February, I spent the tail end of a Saturday afternoon sitting in my kitchen mending a pair of coveralls. It was starting to get dark, and I was listening to a Joan Baez album from the earlier days. The mood held me so strongly that I didn't get up to turn on any lights. The sunset lasted for over an hour, changing from peach to blood to lilac; as the sun slipped in the southwest, the changing colors lit up higher levels of clouds, which in turn were shifting upwards from layers to wisps. It was a rich sunset, common for this country and this time of year, but I wasn't usually so deliberate as to sit and watch it all the way through. When the sky had gone pitchy beyond color, I sat in the dark and listened to an album of classical Spanish guitar. The music seemed louder with the lights off.

It was on this evening, as I sat there weighing past against present, that time revealed itself in a new way. Up until then, I had more or less envisioned my life as one continuous whole—sort of like history in God's eye, as one of my history profs once put it, in which all events in history were always happening, simultaneously. Christ was eternally hanging on the cross, President Kennedy was eternally lurching in his open limousine, Muhammad Ali was eternally regaining and regaining his heavyweight crown. From that viewpoint I saw myself continually awakening to the sun shining through Peggy's window; giving the finger to Fort Benning, Georgia, from the Greyhound window; barbecuing for Marilyn and the kids; singing "Philadelphia Lawyer" with Tom.

On this evening, maybe because Peggy had come back into my life on different terms, or maybe because I had become melancholy watching the sun set, I had a clearer sense of things done and gone. My life with Marilyn Hartlund seemed neatly packed away, like all the packages of a side of beef, tucked into wire baskets and stacked in cold storage for someone who would never pick up the key. Once I saw that much, I could not escape the idea that other pasts were past as well. I could not reach back over the gap and lead Peggy forward, to stand her younger self by mine.

Then I took comfort in recalling what a pretty sunset it had been and, the cold weather notwithstanding, in realizing that the days were getting longer.

* * * * *

As the days moved into late winter, the weather became fickle. Here on the high plains, in view of the Laramie Range, the weather can vary by forty or fifty degrees from one day to the next, so that the country roads are slush and gumbo one day and frozen ruts the next. When the weather was decent at all, I worked with the horses—currying, combing, trimming, and riding. I wanted things to be right for Peggy if she could visit. I received a couple of letters from her, which were mainly accounts of how uninspiring her job was or how mundane the city seemed. Naturally I wanted more, but I knew she had teaching duties and an apartment lease, neither of which she could walk out on. I wrote back, not in the style of the Chamber of Commerce trying to lure more commerce, but trying to make the cold and solitude seem interesting.

One evening as I was cleaning house—I kept it more or less tidy most of the time now, just for practice—the phone rang.

"How's the weather out there?"

"Peggy! It's nice to hear your voice."

"Thought I'd call to check on the weather."

"That's nice of you. Right now it's so-so—overcast but not cold. It can go either way, though. It was pretty warm here about a week ago. How's the weather out your way? Things should be coming into leaf about now, shouldn't they?"

"A little bit, as much as I've noticed. It's been rainy and then sunny, back and forth."

"How are things in general?"

"Oh, fair. Say, the reason I'm calling is that it looks as if I'll be out in your neck of the woods, as they say, in a couple of weeks, and I was wondering if you'd be in the mood for visitors."

"Plural?"

"No. Singular. I meant one visitor."

"More would be fine, too, but, sure. By all means."

"It looks like I'll be leaving here on March 18th."

"Aside from the fact that there's not many trees here, what part of the . . . uh . . . my neck of the woods are you going to?" My heartbeat had picked up.

"I have a conference in Denver. It's a convention for English teachers."

"Are you going to nominate a political candidate?"

"No, it's one of those deals where the good old boys and girls get to hobnob and politic, and the up-and- coming talent like myself look for career openings."

"Oh, so you have some job interviews?"

"One. And it's standard procedure to pick up other interviews at the conference."

"You got time off from your work?"

"Yes. I had to arrange a substitute for one class, but I got time off."

"Are you flying in?"

"Yes. I should get there about 6:00 on the evening of the 18th."

"I could get off early and meet you then." I felt that I sounded too eager, especially when I heard her say, "Oh, no." I backed up quickly. "Unless—"

"No, I mean I'm staying in Denver that night. I have an interview the next day after lunch. That gives me time to look around for other openings."

I thought of offering to meet her there and hang around, but I wasn't sure how to put it. I sat there, wordless.

"So I thought," she continued, "if this sounds all right, I thought I would rent a car and take a drive up your way."

"On the 19th." I was looking at my kitchen calendar.

"Right."

"And when do you fly back out?"

"On the 22nd."

"So you might be here for as long as three days."

"Possibly that long. That depends on what other interviews I can raise."

"Oh. I see. Well, any length of time would be fine. I'll be scheming on how to entertain you. Like I mentioned in my last letter, I've been working with the horses. If the weather is nice, we can ride."

"That sounds . . . interesting. I haven't been on a horse in a long, long time."

"You'll do fine."

"Is there anything I can bring?"

"Hmmm. Yes, there is. What would you think of bringing your guitar?"

"Gee, I, um . . . I'm not sure."

"It's safe enough, isn't it? That is, to ship it?"

"Well, that's not quite the point." She paused. "Roger is driving me to the airport."

"Oh." I went silent again.

"Ken?"

"Yeah. I'm still here."

"Ken, I'd like to stay at least a couple of days. I'll try to set things up that way."

My mouth was dry, but I managed to say, "I'd like you to stay as long as you can."

"I'm looking forward to it, Ken."

"I can't tell you how—um—how excited this has got me."

"Ken."

"Yes?"

"Is there anything else I can bring?"

I thought for a moment. "How about some California wine?"

"Red or white?"

"One of each. Or either. Your choice."

"I think I can manage that. By the way, do I need directions on how to get there?"

"Well, if you're getting in here after five, the easiest way would be to call me from town. Then I can give you directions."

"O.K. See you on the evening of the 19th, then. If anything changes, I'll give you a call."

"O.K., Peggy."

"Bye."

"See you then."

The first thing I did when I hung up was get a long drink of water. Then I put on a winter coat and hat, cut an apple in half, put on some gloves, and went out to give the horses a pep talk.

* * * * *

I heard no more from her, so I assumed there hadn't been any change in plans. As the days gnawed themselves away, I thought more than I needed to about Roger—what he looked like, how much he knew (apparently not much), how much she wanted to protect things with him (apparently at least a little). That line of speculation was generally as productive as guessing which way the Wyoming wind would blow next.

* * * * *

The 19th came, as sure as any other day is bound to come. I arranged to have the next two days off, so I worked through to quitting time and streaked home to do my chores and pick up any little ends I might have missed. All in a moment the call came, and then she was coming down the drive and parking her rented car. It was a tan Cavalier, about as nondescript a car as I imagined she might show up in. She had a suitcase in one hand and a bouquet of mixed fresh flowers in the other, so I didn't hug her right away. I put the flowers into water as she slipped out of her coat, and there she was, trim in a wool sweater and skirt. I had a fleeting thought that she looked like the yuppies she dreaded, but I closed my eyes and took her close to me, buried my face in her hair as I kissed her neck and smelled that faint smell that meant only Peggy— Peggy of Reno, Peggy of college days, Peggy who now stood in my living room and held me to her as she exhaled into my collar.

As we relaxed and moved apart, I half-asked, "I hope you haven't had dinner."

"Not a bite. What's on the menu?"

"Some little Cornish game hens, stuffed. And a salad."

"Supermarket stuff?"

"Tonight."

"Then we'll want the white wine," she announced, and opened the suitcase she had flung on the couch. I had a side view of her posture as she bent over, rummaging where she had wedged the bottles among clothes. She tossed her hair back and looked over her shoulder at me. She smiled, sashayed her butt, and hauled out a bottle of Sebastiani Mountain Rhine.

I asked her if she had anything else to bring in.

"Nothing that can't wait," she said. "What's the best way to chill this?"

"The best way, when the weather is colder, is to put it out on the porch. Tonight, we'll use the freezer compartment."

It was difficult for me, through dinner, not to make comparisons between the girl I knew then and the woman with me now. She still ate chicken with her fingers, but now she put her napkin in her lap. Her smiles and half-frowns seemed deeper; the lines that were once traces were now etched. When we had shoved the plates aside, she looked at me across her wine glass just as she had done on the train and, unless my memory has improved upon time, just as she did in the days before men walked on the moon.

That evening we danced. One album I thought she'd like was by Merle Haggard and Leona Williams together. "Waltz Across Texas" came on, and I thought of the vast desert that had lain between, or joined, her and me.

"I could waltz a long way with you," I said. "How far would you want me to?"

"It would have to be flat."

"Between your place and mine there's some pretty flat stretches," I said. She put her head against my shoulder, and I could feel she was picking up the melody and the emotion of the song. "You came up from Denver. Colorado's not flat. Nevada and Utah are."

"Nevada has Reno," she objected.

"You're right. But most of Utah is flat as a bitch."

"We could waltz across Utah, then, or part of it."

"Yeah. The salt flats. Actually," I mused, "it's a pretty flat desert from Salt Lake all the way to Reno. We could waltz across the desert."

"Yes," she said, "but 'Utah' fits into the rhythm of the line better." She slipped her arms around my neck and kissed me, and we were quiet again.

We listened to the song two more times, and then we turned out the lights.

* * * * *

In the morning I brought in her garment bag and a little canvas shoulder bag that worked as a briefcase, and I left them along with her suitcase in the bedroom. I went to work fixing sausage, eggs, toast, and coffee. It occurred to me that she might have given up red meat somewhere along the way; then I wondered why I made myself worry.

She came out wearing boots, blue jeans, and a heavy wool sweater. "Smells good," she said. Putting a crumble of sausage in her mouth, she asked, "Pork?"

"No, antelope."

"Good for you."

"Part One of your wild west experience."

114

"And in Part Two we ride the range?"

"You betcha."

It turned out to be a halfway decent day to ride, clear but a little windy. I rode Babe and she rode Punky, the gelding. Everything went fine, and toward the end we even loped for about a quarter of a mile. When I had unsaddled the horses, brushed them and turned them into the corral to roll in the dust, she said, "That was terrific. I hope the weather is nice enough again tomorrow."

That night it snowed, about three inches of wet, heavy spring snow. The whole countryside was blanketed with fresh, clean whiteness the next morning, and the day cleared off so that we could ride after lunch.

We went to bed fairly early, and between then and the time we went to sleep, we had the conversation that I had hoped for and dreaded.

Making something like small talk, I said, "It's too bad you have to leave in the morning." She had scheduled an interview for the last day of the convention.

"Uh-huh."

"But I realize you have to look out for your career."

"Yeah," she said, "there *is* sort of an irony there."

"How do you mean?"

"Well, I have to leave you to see about a job that might bring me closer."

"Because the job opening is in Colorado. You'd take the job if you were offered it, wouldn't you?"

"I generally don't apply for a job that I would refuse. From what I know of it so far, yes, I'd take it."

Now came my part. I felt anxiety crowding in. "And if you weren't offered it? Would you feel that you had any other decisions?"

"About . . . ?"

"Well, about your career, or about your personal life, either one."

I could tell she was forming her answer carefully. "Ken, I hope you don't think I came here just on a lark, like your typical conventioneer on a spree."

"Well, no, I didn't. You seem to have taken an interest in things here. How things operate."

"I have."

"Well, that's more or less why I asked my question."

"About decisions."

"Yes, only more like . . . whether you might be back for another visit . . . or a longer stay . . ."

"What if it were the other way around?"

"What do you mean?" I asked. "I don't exactly follow you."

"Would you pack up and move for me?"

That just about floored me, except that I was already lying down. "Hmmm," I said, "I hadn't even thought of that. I have everything here—a job, a place— well, you know, you've taken a look at it."

She put her arm across my chest and snuggled close. She kissed me on the shoulder and said, "I don't mean to be critical. I know that life is very safe and solid for you here. It has been. For a long time. I wouldn't expect you to leave it. So if I did decide to come for a longer visit, I'd be taking a much bigger chance. Than you."

I picked my way with care. "I see what you mean. You'd be giving up . . . whatever you had going for you on the west coast."

"Not that it's all that much," she returned, "but I *would* be taking a risk."

"Can you see yourself staying here, though?"

"Oh, yes. It's utopian. I'd have plenty of peace and quiet to work on my own projects, my expenses would be low, and the company would be . . . 'mighty fine.'"

I smiled. "Sunsets are nice, too."

"I guess," she continued, "I guess it just seems a little too easy. Right now I feel ready for a change, but I might not always want to be secluding myself from the world and all of that."

"So," I ventured, "that's a risk that I would share, more or less automatically—that if you did come, you might not stay."

"What if you took that risk knowingly, or willingly, and not just automatically?"

"I think I could rise to the occasion." I put my left arm under her neck and draped my right arm across her waist. "Peggy, I love you."

"I know you do." She turned toward me. "And I want to do the best thing I can to honor that."

* * * * *

The next morning we had a cheerful breakfast without rehashing the topic from the night before. In the cold clear light of morning, I still felt willing to take a chance with her, so before we carried out her bags, I said so, simply.

"My thoughts are the same, too," she said, and we kissed.

Outside, it promised to be a clear day, balanced between warm and cold. Her car had absorbed enough of the previous afternoon's sun to melt the snow that had covered it, but the air had been chilly enough to freeze the dripping water into icicles that stretched from the under edges of the car to the snow on the ground. There was ice in the door cracks, too.

When she drove away, she left a bare spot in the driveway, the size of her car, with a border of icicles sticking up from the surrounding carpet of snow. She turned onto the main road and drove out of sight. Then the emptiness struck me.

I went in and poured another cup of coffee, but I was drawn to the window to gaze again at the empty patch of driveway and the icicles with broken tops. As I listened to the radio and washed the dishes, it came to me. I was thinking of Marilyn's saddle.

On the last day of her life, on a late winter day, I had come out to the place to saddle our horses for a ride. I had saddled Punky for Marilyn, and I was just brushing Babe when Brad came roaring out in his car. He looked terrified. "Jump in!" he said. "They took Mom to the hospital."

I put Babe in the corral, yanked the saddle off Punky and set it on the top rail of the corral, and shoved Punky in with Babe.

I didn't get back until the next morning, after I had made arrangements with the funeral home and the pastor, and after I had spent a sleepless night with Brad and Kerry. That next morning when I came out to check on the horses, the saddle was still sitting on the corral, and a skiff of overnight snow had settled like dust on the saddle. I have never had such a concentrated feeling of emptiness, but on this later morning, after Peggy had left me, I was haunted by that earlier feeling.

* * * * *

For the next two weeks, I waited for a letter or a phone call from Peggy, but I got neither. For a few days, I noticed, the phone didn't ring at all. Then for a stretch of about four evenings, I was plagued by telephone solicitors selling magazine subscriptions and supper club memberships, trying to renew service warranties, wondering if I'd gotten their brochure in the mail for the investment property in South Dakota. Sometimes it seems as if that kind of junk communication comes in waves or phases, like mail order advertisements and life insurance offers. If any of those honest-working, underpaid phone solicitors had known how much I wanted the phone to ring and how little I wanted to hear their line, they probably would have cut it shorter.

At last I received a letter from her, a short letter, telling me she didn't get the first job she had interviewed for, but she was still in the running for the second one, as far as she knew. She spoke briefly of warm weather and the drudgery of grading papers, both of which seemed a long ways away, and she conveyed best wishes to Babe and Punky. She signed it "Love Peg" and added a P.S. to tell me she was learning our waltz song on the guitar.

That evening as I was washing dishes and assuring myself that it was indeed the first time she'd closed a letter that way, the phone rang. As I dried my hands, I shook off the possibility that it might be her, on the heels of her letter. It sure as hell wasn't.

"Is this Ken Thomas?" The voice sounded antagonistic.

"That's me. Speaking."

"This is Roger Morgan."

I didn't say anything.

"Peg's boyfriend," he pushed.

"O.K. I know who you are."

"I called up to let you know you could do us all a big favor by minding your own business."

"Did Peggy give you my number?"

"No, I—don't worry how I got your number. I'm just telling you to mind your own business."

I was getting mad fast, that kind of mad where my stomach churns and I start shaking. My voice cracks then, too, so I cleared my throat (in his ear, I hoped) and said, "I doubt that you have the nerve to be calling with her sitting there. If you want to know what the cards are, ask her. Don't call me up and try to bully me."

"Look here, buddy, I got one thing to say to you."

"Say it and hang up, or I will."

"You're just damn lucky you live as far away as you do, or I'd drop by and kick your ass up between your shoulder blades."

"Anything else?"

"Just that."

"Well, keep hoping." And I hung up. Boy, I was mad. I was sure he'd gotten my name and address off an envelope and was calling from his place, wherever that was. I had even less of an image of that than I did of him. I started to dial her number, but

I hung up halfway through. I was too mad, and besides, I had just gotten her letter that said, more or less, to hang on. So I finished the dishes and brooded.

With some effort, I could imagine how he felt. If I was in danger of losing a woman like her to a guy he probably imagined me to be, some chump out on the plains, I think I would be provoked, too. Then it occurred to me that he might be feeling desperate and might have good reason to. I took heart at that thought, wiped up the drainboard, and poured a bourbon and water. By the end of the second one, I was able to think of him as someone who lived in a different world, in a world where women read fascinating novels about cavewomen and went to the casinos to play blackjack and slot machines and then went to the smoky lounge where they could dance to the electric music of Roger and His Ilk. I hoped he would meet one of those women; in that way he might be able to play caveman and not have to bother any more with this old shitkicker.

* * * * *

The call from Roger came on Tuesday, the second week of April. By the next Friday, I hadn't heard from her again, so I went to happy hour with a crowd from work. There was very little worth noting in this except that in the process, I forgot to pick up my mail on the way home.

By the time I put my feet on the floor the next morning, the sun was shining warm and handsome. I had a late breakfast and decided to ride Punky. It was his turn. As I brushed him, I mentioned to him that I hoped I wouldn't always be the one to ride him. Then we went on a jaunt.

The new grass was up about an inch and a half or so, in many places poking through the old grey grass that had flattened beneath the winter snows. What little snow was left was cached in the shadiest clefts of draws and ditches. It was a fragile time of the year, a brief time of promise that the bad weather was over or almost over and that the warmer weather would soon set in. The horses were starting to shed their winter coats. Before long the thin, bristly canes of the wild rose would leaf out. The tapering scarlet buds would follow, and they would open into smiling pink blossoms. By then the rattlesnakes would be out, and not long after that, the cactus would be in bloom. I could plant my garden and worry about hail-storms, sit in the sunrise shadow of my barn to drygulch rabbits on their way to my beans. Life and its counterparts would be in full swing.

Punky and I took the long way down by the corn stubble and hay fields, along the government canal, and back along the sunny side of a row of elms not yet come into leaf. Rather than turn back to the barn, where Punky wanted to go, I took the gravel to the main road, to my mailbox. I was nervous. To put off my possible disappointment, I picked the gravel and earth out of Punky's hooves. Then I opened the mailbox and drew out a letter.

Dear Ken, it said.

Sorry to take so long to write, but I've been waiting every day to get something in the mail about the second job. To-

day I got the letter which told me, to their regret, that they had chosen another candidate.

My mouth was dry. I read on.

Meanwhile, I have come to the conclusion that I'm not getting any further where I am, and a change might do me good. So if you still think you can handle the risk, I think I'll pull up stakes here. Isn't that the way we say it out west?

When she was here, she had kidded me about travelling more than a thousand miles east to reach the west.

I was starting to feel giddy as I read on.

School finishes for me at the end of May, and I'll have a few things to tidy up—put some stuff in storage, and that sort of thing. I think it's only fair to tell you that I may come back here at the end of the summer, even though I don't plan to right now. I'll be keeping in touch as time draws nearer. Right now I am snowed under (so to speak) with school work, so this will be brief.

I look forward to my stay. I have very fine thoughts about last month's visit. Call me if you want— I'm the only one who answers the phone here. And give my best to Babe and Punky. See you soon.

Love Peg.

The remark about the telephone struck me funny. For one thing, I had never called her, probably because I *was* afraid she wouldn't be alone. Also buried in there somewhere was a hint, I thought, about me and Roger and the telephone. But I didn't give a damn about that. Life was too big, the sun too warm, for me to worry. Yes, I thought, I could damn sure handle the risk.

My head was all a-swirl, but I had the presence of mind to check Punky's cinch. I patted him on the neck and said out loud, "You betcha, boy." I swung into the saddle and turned him homewards, and as Punky picked up a brisk walk back to the barn, I sang a loud and happy version of "Philadelphia Lawyer." Tom's version.

He Knew it, Too

A man emerged from the crowd around the bar and stopped at Allen and Carolyn's table. His face was in shadow as he said, "You're Allen Fields, aren't you?"

"That's right."

"You remember me?"

Allen studied the man who stood in front of him—a man with a slight build, in loose-fitting clothes, long stringy hair hanging out beneath a baseball cap, and bad teeth showing in his friendly smile. The man choked a long-neck Budweiser in one hand and held a cigarette with an inch-long ash in the other. Allen shook his head in hesitation. He knew he should recognize the man, but he couldn't quite place him.

"Joe Parnell." The man stuck the cigarette in his mouth and thrust his hand forward.

A scene from years earlier flashed in Allen's mind. He stood up, shook Joe's hand, and invited him to join them. Joe took a seat. Allen introduced Joe and Carolyn to each other. As Allen sat down, he felt an uneasiness spread through his upper body.

"Your husband's one good sumbitch."

Carolyn nodded and smiled at the compliment.

Joe took a swig of his beer, and still grasping the bottle by the neck, he held it against his thigh. He fumbled his cigarette from his mouth as he brought his gaze to settle on Allen. "Buy you two a drink?"

"No, thanks, Joe. We just stopped in for one drink on our way home from supper. We've got to get home."

"Be glad to buy you a drink."

"Some other time. But thanks."

"O.K." Parnell flicked his ashes on the floor, took a long drag on his cigarette, and snuffed the butt in the ashtray. He shook Allen's hand across the table, then pushed himself up out of his chair and away.

On the way home, Allen told Carolyn the story of how he came to be a good sumbitch. "This guy Joe Parnell, I sort of stuck up for him once, back in high school. It all happened in a minute. We were in the restroom, just before an assembly. Parnell was a scroungy kid that everyone picked on—his clothes never fit him very well, probably second-hand or hand-me-downs, and he didn't tuck in his shirt. You know—a poor kid that no one much cared about. Anyway, on this one day, when the three of us were in the bathroom, another kid kicked Parnell in the ass."

"What for?"

"Because he could get away with it, I guess. Parnell was no-body, and this other kid was jayvee quarterback—part of the in-crowd, and all that."

"Oh. I see."

"This other kid, Roy Carter, was a sophomore. Parnell was a freshman. I was a senior, so I took the privilege of kicking Carter, like he had kicked Parnell. It all happened just like that."

"What did the other boy do when you kicked him?"

"He turned around and looked at me, like he was totally surprised I'd kicked him instead of Parnell. The funny thing was,

I didn't like Parnell any better than the next guy did. But it seemed so unfair, I acted automatically. I told Carter if he wanted to pick on someone, he could pick on me."

"And of course he didn't."

"Of course not. I was already a big farm boy, and a senior, so he just walked away."

Allen fell silent as he recalled the rest of the scene, how he and Parnell had looked at each other just long enough for their eyes to meet and move away. It had been clear that there was no instant friendship and no expectation of gratitude. The whole incident had indeed happened in a minute—two kicks, two glances, a few words, and no mistake about who meant what. The middle boy had probably forgotten it, but the other two hadn't.

Allen turned off the paved road and onto the gravel. "So that's the story. I've never considered him my friend. I've never really cared for him, and tonight I didn't even recognize him at first. I've probably seen him a hundred times since high school, but I don't remember ever talking to him before. And then tonight, out of the blue, he acts like my old friend."

"He didn't say anything about it, did he?"

"No, he just offered to buy us a drink. You heard everything he said."

"He probably admires you. You stuck up for him one time, a long time ago, and he remembers you for it. This is probably his way of thanking you." She laid her hand on his arm. "You should be proud."

The headlights poured two beams against the stuccoed farmhouse as Allen brought the car to a stop. He switched off the headlights and shut off the motor. "I didn't feel like I was sticking up for him, but I guess it amounts to that."

"Well, I'm proud of you. You did the right thing."

Two weeks later, as Carolyn handed Allen the phone and he heard Parnell's voice come over the line, he felt a chill spread through his neck and shoulders. The scene in the bar came to mind, as did the scene from the rest room, like two bubbles touching.

"Well, hello, Joe," he heard himself saying. "How are you doing?"

"Just fine, Allen. And you?"

"Oh, fine."

"And your wife?"

"Oh, she's fine, too." Allen felt a knot tighten in his stomach. Here it comes, he thought. He's going to invite us to something.

"I'll tell you why I called, Allen."

"Uh-huh."

"I was wonderin' if you let people hunt pheasants on your place."

"Well, yeah, we usually do."

"You think there be a chance I could come try my luck?"

"Sure, that would be all right. When would you like to come?"

"Maybe Saturday afternoon. I work till noon."

"That should be okay. I'll be looking for you then."

"Thanks, Allen."

"You bet." Allen stared at the phone after he cradled it.

"Who was that?" Carolyn asked. "You sounded funny."

128

"That was Joe Parnell. You remember—the guy at the bar."

"Oh, yes."

"He wants to come out for some bird hunting. I told him it would be all right. He's coming out Saturday afternoon."

"There shouldn't be anything wrong with that."

"No, I don't think so. He said he works till noon, and he'll be out after that."

On Saturday afternoon, Allen had gotten himself busy at nailing down loose metal siding on the tractor shed by the time Joe pulled into the farm yard. A black Lab in the back of the pickup looked on as the master put on a tan hunting vest and pulled a shotgun from the gun rack. Joe snapped his fingers, and the dog clambered out of the truck. Joe grabbed the dog by the collar and half-dragged it across the yard to check in with Allen. As Joe came closer, Allen saw the smudge and film of automotive work on Joe's shoes, pants, and cap. Beneath the hunting vest, a quilted jacket hung unzipped, with stuffing visible through the battery acid burns. But the man was sober if not clean, and Allen gave him the layout.

From the top of the tractor shed, Allen could see the farm land below. He watched Parnell from time to time, seeing the lone man work the fields and ditches. He heard the man calling to the dog, whose name seemed to be Jip, and a few times he heard the distant *pop* of the twelve-gauge.

The temperature had hovered at just above freezing all afternoon, and it started dropping off at about the time Parnell came in, at dusk. Allen, just finished with chores, was ready to go inside.

"Well, how did you do?"

"Two roosters."

"Good goin'."

"Not too bad. If I was a better shot I'd'a had my limit."

Allen nodded and smiled. Joe stood with the shotgun in the crook of his arm, silence lingering in the cold air. It was only polite to ask him in. "Would you like to go inside for a minute or so?"

Joe hesitated. "Sure. Why not. Let me put these things away."

As Joe walked to the pickup, Allen noticed a rooster tail sticking out of each side of the bulging back pouch. Joe pounded on the bed of the pickup, and the Lab jumped up over the green fender well and into the bed. Allen watched as Joe poked the shotgun into the rack, pulled the two roosters out of the pouch, and tossed them onto the passenger's floorboard. Joe's breath was clouding in the air as he walked to the house.

Allen led the way into the small front room of the farm house. Showing his guest to a chair by the wood-burning stove, he said, "I can offer you coffee, Pepsi, or beer."

Joe looked up and smiled. "I drink a beer."

Allen didn't keep much beer on hand. "Pabst all right?"

"Fine with me."

Joe thanked Allen for the beer, popped the top, took a short sip, and licked his mustache. Then he took a long swallow. The two men sat for two or three minutes without speaking.

Carolyn came from the kitchen, with Tessie half-hiding behind her. "Well, did you have any luck?"

Parnell looked at her and smiled, showing his decayed teeth more clearly than in the dark bar. "I shoot two nice roosters.

Nice ones. I bet they have their craws full of corn when I clean 'em." He looked at the little girl, peeping blue-eyed at him. "And what's your name?"

Tessie hid her face in her mother's leg.

"C'mon, now, what's your name?"

Carolyn patted her on the head and said, "Tell him."

The girl looked out and said, "Tessie."

"Tessie what?"

"Tessie Lynn Fields."

"And how old are you, Tessie?"

"Foh-er."

"Foh-er? I gotta little girl that's foh-er, too, just like you. I bet you and her would be real good friends." Tessie buried her head again, and Parnell looked at Carolyn. "Mrs. Fields, I give you one of them roosters if you like."

"Oh, no, thank you. We get plenty. You take yours home to your own wife. Does she like pheasant?"

"Oh, yeah. She cook everything I bring home."

"Well, you take yours home. We can get as many as we ever want, can't we, Allen?"

"Of course we can. I don't go out and hunt much, but if we want pheasant, we can have it." Allen looked at Joe, trying to imagine what kind of a wife he might have.

Tessie spoke up. "What's your little girl's name?"

"Tara. Tara Ann. And she just loves her daddy. I bet you love your daddy, too, don't you?" Joe smiled a relaxed, lazy smile, as if the beer was taking effect already.

Allen, watching Carolyn put her arm around Tessie, asked, "What's your wife's name, Joe?"

"Jolene. Maybe you knew her. Jolene Mills."

"Oh, uh-huh." Allen remembered having seen them once, maybe a year earlier, at the grocery store. There had been Joe, the stout wife, and a couple of kids, none of them immaculate. As the clerk rang up the groceries, Joe had gone over to lean on a stack of bagged potatoes, where he had lit a cigarette and loitered. Allen remembered wondering why the man, whom he dimly recognized at the time, kept aloof. Then the wife had pulled out an envelope full of food stamps, and it had all made sense.

"Yep. Got two little kids. Little Tara Ann, she's four, and a little boy comin' on three. Tyson's his name." Joe smiled at Allen and said, "He's a ornery little shit."

Allen nodded. "We've just got Tessie so far." He looked over toward his wife and daughter in time to see them vanishing into the kitchen.

The two men sat for a moment longer until Joe drained his beer and stood up. "Well, I think I better move along." He set his beer can on the chair and yawned and stretched. "I sure thank you for lettin' me hunt your place. And for the beer."

"Well, it's just fine. I hope you can come again."

Carolyn appeared from the kitchen. "Allen, be sure he takes some pumpkins."

Joe turned to her.

"Pumpkins. We had a good garden this year, and we're trying to give them away. Does your wife use pumpkin?"

"I think so, for bread and pies, prob'ly."

"Well, take at least a couple."

132

Joe looked at Allen, who nodded and said, "We've got a lot of pumpkins. We had a good crop of them."

Later that evening, as Allen and Carolyn stood side by side washing and rinsing the supper dishes, she asked, "Did Joe take two pumpkins?"

"Huh? Oh, yeah. I made sure he took two."

"Good. Between that and the pheasants, his wife might be a little happier this evening."

Allen shrugged. "If he's home yet."

"What do you mean?"

"Oh, I'd bet a quarter he stopped at some bar on the way home." Allen imagined the dog sitting in the back of the pickup with the two pumpkins, and the birds growing cold and stiff in the cab.

"Well, maybe he did." She bumped him with her hip. "What's the matter?"

"Oh, nothing, really. It was just sort of funny, sitting there and both of us knowing we weren't really friends."

"He knew it, too, didn't he?"

"I think so."

"Allen?"

"Yeah?"

"Did he make you uncomfortable while he was inside the house here?"

"I think so. Did he you?"

"Yes, he did. When Tessie was there."

"Yeah."

"But, still, you know, Allen, I don't think there's any harm in him."

"Oh, no, I think you're right."

"Does he live with his wife and kids?"

"I'm pretty sure he does, from the way he talked. And I've seen them together, shopping."

"He's just a little . . . unsavory. He's not going to contaminate anybody, though."

"No, he's O.K. He's just different, that's all. I told him he could come out and hunt again."

"That was nice."

Allen held a handful of glowing white soap suds, glanced at his wife, and smiled.

"Don't you dare," she said.

"Dare what?"

"I know what you're thinking. You want to poof those suds on me."

"And you love it," he said, doing just that, slapping the soap suds on her butt as they met for a kiss. When they drew apart, he looked her close in the eyes and said, "You know what else I was thinking?"

She shook her head.

"I was thinking how nice it was of you to offer him the pumpkins."

Pearl, Shadow and Light

That first summer we were married she cut off her hair, had it cut off a little at a time. We were broke, living in a basement apartment, and she found it depressing. So she cut off her hair and tried to get pregnant.

"It's okay," I said. "Get your hair cut the way you want. If you don't like the way it looks, you can let it grow back."

"I feel like a miserable mole, living down in this hole," she would say. Then we would make love and she would tell me, crying, "What I want most of all, more than anything, is to have your baby."

Words like that made me feel better, even if we weren't set up for baby. I had just gone back to work, and we were more or less agreed that we would do house, baby, and car, in that order. Now she was pushing baby first, maybe both house and baby at once, I wasn't sure. But if it made her happy, I could adjust. And it was exciting to try for baby.

Some of it was my fault, in a way—the part about not having a better place to live. The summer before, when we were engaged, I was living in the mobile home. One Saturday afternoon she drove out to see me while I was working in the yard, transplanting some young shade trees to what was to be the back yard. We sat in the shade of the mobile home and drank beer, cold bottled beer in the warm shade. I set the water running to soak the trees in their new places, and I thought about the holes

I would have to go back and fill in where I had dug up the trees in the windbreak.

She was thinking about the mobile home. "What's going to become of this thing?"

"Oh, I think we could live in it for a while, until we get the house built."

"And where does the house go?"

She already knew. I'd told her more than once. I still harbored the plan I'd started with Stephanie—to build an earth-sheltered home down the hill a ways. It was what anyone would want, a southern exposure and out of the wind somewhat.

So I said, "Down over there."

And she said, "No, I don't want to live in the ground. I want the house here."

"Right here?"

"Right here. Where this thing is."

"What kind of a house, then?"

"A regular house. A *normal* house."

I looked at the little trees and said, pointing with my thumb, "Then I take it you don't want to live in this thing." She knew, as I had told her, that two people could live in it.

"If you don't get rid of it, I won't marry you." Those were her words as we sat in the warm shade, drinking cold beer, on that Saturday afternoon.

Looking back, I could ask, what drove me to it? Why would I find myself, months later, as the wind blew and the snowflakes fell, helping strangers rip out the skirting, cut the roots of water supply and sewer hook-up, take down the fence, and jockey that long awkward crate off of my property and on down the road?

Partly it was because I wanted to get along. I was living in the shadow of failure from my first marriage, and I didn't want to hear again that I was too hard to get along with.

Partly it was because she had already set the pattern, earlier, that she would have things as she wanted. After we had been going out for a couple of months, she decided we should just be friends—meaning, we wouldn't sleep together anymore. Then, a month and a half later, she decided we could be lovers again. I was thrilled. In another three months I was engaged. Looking back, I think that pattern set me up for getting rid of the mobile home, even though at the time I imagined I was trying not to be too hard to get along with. So I overdid it the other way, and I made it too easy for her to get her way.

I got rid of the trailer, took an apartment in town, got married as planned, got laid off in the dead of winter, and ended up living in a hole in the ground anyway.

It was dark and cool down in the basement, so we could go to bed early on those summer evenings. The awareness of baby was a dimension I hadn't known before, something that had never come around with Stephanie, and even if I wasn't quite ready for it in my own sense of order, it was a strong pull. "I want to have your baby." The words of the Indian princess.

Even with her long black hair cut off, she was the dark earth to me—child of the earth, and earth itself. I wasn't just making love with my wife. I was mingling with all of it: ravens, horses, juniper trees, clear water, desert sun. Her adoptive parents vanished, and she was the Indian princess, anonymous, without personal connections or attachments. Child of the earth, orphan—wild dark fruit by nature, pale Hoosier by nurture.

When we tried for baby, the midwesterners were gone from the picture.

Thinking of the children that would be, I imagined them with her features—quick dark eyes, aquiline nose, thick rich hair. Smart, mannered kids, like their mother, they would also have the spirit, the straight line back to the desert. The heat and the strength of the ancient sun would flow in their blood. That was my picture.

I think some of her depression came from the change in hormones from going off the pill, and I think some of it came from baby's failure to become. Some of it came, no doubt, simply because things weren't going her way. I thought she might cheer up if she got a job; we could certainly use the money.

"I'm not going back to waiting tables," she said. "My parents didn't put me through college for that."

"It's okay," I said. "We're getting by." We were.

After work I would go out to the place, usually by myself, and take care of the horse and the plant life. Several months after the trailer was gone, a friend brought out his tractor and helped me root out the cement footings, so there was a long, bare depression surrounded by new trees, lilac bushes, lawn, and flower beds. It was a bit odd by some standards, to have a hole in the midst of a well-kept yard, but it was a pretty place that summer. We set a campfire pit in the low spot, and we had a couple of picnics there. We also camped, one weekend.

We were sitting by the campfire, appreciating out loud the simplicity of it all, having fun with the idea that I was a ten-percent cowboy and she was half Indian. Eventually we got to the point where I held my hand in front of my face, palm inward, separated my fingers two-and-two into a vee, squinted through, and claimed, "I could find you in the dark."

She stuck out her tongue and winked in the firelight. "You're just a pony soldier. You're no scout."

The upshot of it was that she went into the tent and came out wrapped in only a blanket, a cotton sarape we used for a bed cover. I would have ten minutes, with my eyes closed, to find her. She was free to move around, but both of us would stay on all fours. I was in my underwear. She claimed to have a better sense of time than I did, so she would tell me when the game was up.

I started from a corner, imagined a diagonal across the lawn, and decided to cut the field in half, zig-zagging back and forth from my course. If that failed, I would try a circle.

The direct method did fail, so when I felt the lilac bushes poking at my forehead, I started the circle to my left. It was probably a bad circle, but I had a method in mind. I crawled along, trying to keep my ears and nose open. My original joke was that I could sniff her out in the dark, but she had taken off her smoky clothes, so I had to listen for the whisper of the blanket on the grass.

After a while I heard it, and then again. I scrambled, turned, scrambled, and lunged—and caught the fringe of the sarape. Then I came to her, hand over hand, crawling with my eyes still closed, finding and confirming, then conforming, mingling with her softness as the campfire crackled in the background.

"May I open my eyes now?"

"Go ahead."

"How did I do?"

"Not bad for a pony soldier."

* * * * *

Still no baby, through that summer and into the fall. She counseled with her mother, conferred with the baby doctor. She continued to hate the basement, and I wondered why the child of the earth would be so set against it, unless the earth had been nurtured out of her. Then I made it a question of nature; I imagined her as the sun princess, rebelling against her confinement.

This princess business was a child of my own imagination, which I clung to long after I had any cause. It came from the story as it came to me from her, as it had come to her. Her mother was Indian, Papago. Her father, unknown, was Anglo. The mother had died and left the baby, alone in this world. A kindly couple, who had raised two boys but had always wanted a girl, adopted her. And here she was now, a grown woman, beautiful, a study in heredity and environment.

This kindly couple, although I call them the Hoosiers, are from Iowa. I could call them corn savages, but they aren't farmers, never were. So I call them Hoosiers—typical midwestern, middle-class palefaces, right down to the four television sets, three cars, and unacknowledged gay son. I am a paleface too, but I don't lie about my family, so I have found my way to describe that difference. Deep down, I'm still bitter about the way they raised the child in a bubble of dishonesty, and I try to make light of it by calling them something they aren't. It's my idea of a joke, I suppose, and maybe not a very good one, since they didn't even have to come from the midwest to be in the bubble manufacturing business.

At about the time I was adjusting to the idea of yanking out the mobile home, my princess was fresh out of college and back home living with mom and dad. Also living with them was mom's youngest brother, Len. He did a little yard work, a little scraping and painting on the house trim; he helped with the kitchen work and watched soap operas with his sister. Mom took care of him because he was her baby brother and because he was just getting by on disability checks for a bad back. He was also trying to stay sober, which he was doing pretty well at.

Along about the middle of the summer, mom and dad and daughter went on a visit back home, to Davenport, Iowa. They left Uncle Len to keep an eye on the house, and me to keep an eye on him.

"He's doing so well," said my wife-to-be. It sounded like her mom, who had probably said it first.

He must have started drinking right after they left. By the time I checked with him the next day, he was on a bender. There was a bottle of vodka on the coffee table, a large triangular glazed ashtray full of stubs, and two crumpled cigarette packs. He offered me one of dad's economy-brand beers, and I accepted.

I had barely gotten started on my beer when he up and told me he was her father. Just like that.

"What do you mean?"

"I'm her father. Jim and Barbara adopted her from inside the family."

"Oh, shit. And she doesn't know?"

"No one knows outside of the family."

"Except me."

"Except you."

"Why did you tell me? That's quite a bomb to lay on me."

"You love her, don't you?"

"Of course I do."

"Well, I thought you should know. And, since you love her, I thought you'd accept it."

It wasn't until weeks later, after he had gone down the road, that I concluded his real motive—to pressure mom and dad into bringing out the truth before the wedding. I think he wanted an end to the long masquerade he'd been drawn into, but he didn't have the nerve to do the unveiling himself. So he rigged it. He told me, he told his sister he told me, and then he left. He was a Hoosier, too.

In the course of that afternoon, that strange afternoon in the stale, curtained living room, he told me assorted stories and facts while I drank half a dozen of those cheap beers. The mother was still alive. She was a drunk, just as he was. My wife-to-be had brothers and sisters scattered all over, from Len's first marriage, the mother's first marriage, and their time together. Three of the children had been adopted out of the family. One of the girls was dead, and one of the boys was in prison. Len showed me a scar on his stomach that, according to his story, came from a fight in Oklahoma; they buried the other man, and they put Len in prison for a few years. That was in between marriages.

So here I was, engaged to be married, trying to sell my mobile home, sitting on a twenty-three-year-old family secret, and wondering when it was going to break. While I wondered, I came to understand how such a secret kept on going. Part of it was to protect little brother, and part of it was to shield the baby from the truth that was all around her. Once mom and dad committed themselves to the lie, they kept it up, covering the truth with layer after layer of pampering. They spoiled her rotten, gave her every single thing she wanted, so that if and when the truth ever broke, they could say, as they eventually did, "We did it because we loved you."

In the meanwhile, she learned that when she put her pretty little foot down, she got away with it. It was a strange pattern, to pamper a baby and nurture a tyrant. And I had become part of the pattern long before I realized it.

It was an ugly scene, as she recounted it to me, that day the truth came to light. It is a small part in this story about the search for baby, but it was a major event in my wife's life. After she had been ravaged by the truth and had thrown a dark fit in return, she came to see me. We were in the process of ordering wedding invitations. It was one of the last evenings I spent in the trailer; the weather was cold and wet and bleak as we sat on the sofa in the living room. I hugged her and patted her beautiful black hair as she choked out the story. Really, she told two stories together—the trauma of that afternoon, and the secret of long ago. Most of the latter I had already heard, and now we put our versions together.

"Did he tell you what my name was before I was adopted?"

"No. What was it?"

"Pearl. My name was Pearl."

I had mixed feelings in all of this. On one hand I despised the Hoosiers for their lying and their over-protectiveness. I thought they should have let her grow more naturally into what she would be. It seemed to me that they had spoiled the child of the earth, shaped her into a stupid clay pot, and yet I knew, at the same time, that the orphan princess was a form of my own devising, and she was half Hoosier after all.

As I say, I hung on to this picture for a longer time than was called for—on through the first year of marriage and all our struggles to find baby. It was still with me when spring came a second time upon our bare parcel of land. One afternoon in May, I was moving those same young shade trees again, after their two-year stay, to make room for the house we would build and then fight over. I was down in the hole, wrapping burlap around the ball of dirt and roots, when she drove up. I wrestled the tree out of the earth and laid it, horizontally, on the ground.

"Congratulations," she said. "You're going to be a daddy."

Cautious optimism, to say the least. Through all our troubles in bringing baby together, we had learned that my wife's reproductive system was imperfectly developed, possibly as the result of her own mother's drinking during pregnancy. This imperfect system, we understood, could bring grief at any point along the way.

By now I was used to being uncertain about how I ought to feel. Through one crisis after another, we focused on her feelings and more or less set mine aside. Now there was a promise of baby. I was supposed to be happy, but there was such a cloud over us that I couldn't let myself go. It was a good thing I didn't, because when the miscarriage came, I didn't have so far to fall. Instead of grief-stricken, I was only numb—numb, I guess, from the pillar-to-post series of events I had been through.

It's not really a blur, that episode. It's a sequence of dull, painful pictures—my wife, pale and terrified; the pastor, explaining that God's way is mysterious; the doctor, assuring us it would turn out all right; her mother, smoking one cigarette after another; then my wife, full of anger and no clear direction to send it, full of grief without a clear object to grieve.

She took it plenty bad. She had really wanted the baby, and now it was lost, a broken promise. None of it made sense to her, she said; and in a broader way, it made no sense to me either.

After a short stay at the hospital, she laid up at her parents' house, where I visited her four times a day. It was an unusual arrangement to me, but it was the way she wanted it.

On one of my visits, she bitched at me for being late. I shrugged and got up to get a cup of coffee in the kitchen. Mom followed me, and as I stirred the cream into the coffee, she said, "Be patient with her. Tammy just needs more love."

The doctors told us we could try again, and when the house was built, we did. But something had changed by then. As I imagined our future children, they no longer looked like quick, dark warriors. They began to look like Hoosiers. Something changed in her, too. I heard it. At some point she had left off saying "your baby" and "our baby." It became "a baby," and later on it was "no baby."

Not ever. Not by birth. Not by adoption. "I just can't do it," she said.

There was more to this than I can claim to understand. I tried to set myself aside, as it seemed I had been doing for a long time, and I tried to grasp how the trauma of miscarriage and the disillusionment of her own adoption had closed two doors in her mind. She was going to have an operation, and that was it. To make sense for myself, I had to see it in terms of what it meant to me. She was getting her way. She was putting her foot down.

"Maybe you'll think differently after a little time has passed. This doesn't have to be a snap decision."

"It's not a snap decision. I've thought about it and thought about it, and I know what I want." We were sitting on the couch in our new living room, and she put her head against my chest. "I just can't, that's all." Then she cried, and I held her tight and stroked her beautiful hair. It was growing back. She moved her head to speak. "Is it all right with you?"

"Of course it's all right with me. These kinds of decisions have to start with you." I patted her hair.

"We're going to be all right, aren't we?"

"Yes," I said, "we're going to be all right," but as I said it, I had the strange new feeling that I was lying. I knew I was trying not to be hard to get along with. And I was beginning to understand what it meant when her mom said she needed more love.

"You know I need someone to take care of me."

"Yes, and you know I've wanted to." I was beginning to realize, that evening as we sat on the sofa, that there would be a child anyway, this child that I held, this child that had been handed from one set of parents to another and then to me. I had hoped that with baby she would grow out of her selfishness and join me as a parent. But she was determined to remain the child, and it was not the child I had grown to look for. That's why I was being so easy to get along with. I knew I needed to find some way out of being a childless parent—or worse, my child's lover.

* * * * *

One of our wedding gifts had been a stoneware vase, something vaguely Indian or Southwestern, I guess. It was in dull earth tones, with a body the shape of a tulip bulb and a neck too narrow to put any reasonable number of flowers in. But it was pleasing to the eye. One day, after we had moved into the house, we found the vase where it had fallen from the oak buffet and broken to pieces. Neither of us had been home all day, and no pets had been inside. As nearly as we could tell, the vase had simply fallen and broken. Maybe vibration from the railroad tracks or from the constant wind had brought it to the edge.

They spoiled her and I failed her, that's how I see it. I had my own mystique to fit onto her, and when that was way gone, as gone as the vase, I gave up on her. I had become her parent when I thought I was her protecting lover, and now that I saw where I was, I didn't want to be there.

Pearl went on to an older man, much older than myself, a man whose kids were already raised. He was her counselor first, and now he takes care of her. As for myself, I sit in the shade of a tree now big enough to reciprocate. I see the diamond and emerald sparkle of the newly watered lawn, and I picture a woman at my side as children frolic in front of us.

On the Wind

Clay stood at the window, looking down the hill to the south. Someone had let a grassfire get out of hand. It looked as if it had started along Mace's fenceline, caught hold of the drain ditch at the foot of Mace's pasture, and then gotten into the cattails and tall grass in the slough. Flames were licking high above the banks—big flames jumping up here and there, with sometimes a sheet of flame that shot up by itself, not connected to the fuel or the rest of the fire. Thick grey smoke billowed up out of the heart of the fire and lifted on the wind, which was blowing west to east, the direction that the slough ran.

Clay expected that the fire would eat its way along the slough, across the bottom of the little valley, and not move up the hill at all. Still, he didn't like it. Every year at this time, between the snow of winter and the green-up of spring, people got the fever to burn their weeds. Farmers were the worst, and now it seemed that Mace, the quarter-horse breeder, was the same way.

"Pretty good fire going on down in the bottom," Clay said.

Cindy spoke from the bed. "I was wondering why you were standing there."

He felt her eyes on him, and he imagined he looked funny if not silly, standing there in his shirt and tie with his bare ass to her, the shirt tail lifting up and out in the front. "I don't know why everyone gets so hot to burn weeds," he said.

"Why don't you just close the curtain."

"In a minute."

As Clay stood turned away from Cindy, he had a sense of her presence, an image of how he had seen her just a couple of minutes earlier, when he had gone to the window. She was in her bra and panties, under the sheet, waiting for him to curtain out the sunlight, leave his shirt and tie on the chair with his jacket, and make good on his threat to jump her bones.

"That sounds like a siren now," she said.

"Uh-huh." After another thirty seconds, Clay saw a fire truck pull into the pasture north of Mace's charred fenceline. "There's a fire truck now." He turned and smiled at her.

She smiled back, and he liked the way her blonde hair lay spread on the pillow.

He pulled the curtain cord and shut out the strongest of the light. With the taste of communion wine still in his mouth, he made quick, neat work of taking off the shirt and tie. Then he slipped under the sheet with his wife, still ready.

She laid her hand on his ribs, just above his waist. "That's my cowboy," she said.

There were times, like right now, when saying and doing the right thing seemed to come to her without effort.

The taste of the wine was clear and even in his mouth, a remnant of the clean feeling he had had as he knelt at the rail and prayed. *Take and drink; this is the true blood of our savior Jesus Christ.* The chalice had been cool as his lips touched it, right where his wife's had been. On the first Sunday of each month, the pastor used the silver goblet instead of the little plastic shot glasses. With sinners of the same family, he did not rotate the cup; when he moved from Clay to the Federspiels, he turned the cup to give them an untouched rim.

Clay held the clean feeling in his mouth as he moved toward Cindy. Every Sunday that they went to church, he carried that feeling home with him, and while they were changing clothes in the sunlit bedroom, he felt the urge to make more of it. But he had always held back. His friend Brad, who had dated a female minister, told him a story from that lady. According to her, it was common for men to want to have sex with her. "Rape a nun" was her figure of speech for what they seemed to want. Clay, for all his wanting to love his own wife, felt chastised in advance. He hadn't dared suggest it, not in all the Sundays of coming home from the church they'd been married in two years earlier. Today he had dared, and from her playful answer that he ought to try it, he knew the self-accusation was more his problem than hers.

She had been born into the Lutheran church, baptized and brought up in that same place, so that when she took communion, she went all the way. He, too, felt clean as he partook, but he didn't yet know how to give himself over completely. He always knew, as he left the railing and later as he went to the bedroom (and usually right back out), that he carried the actual taste of wine in his mouth.

They kissed, and her mouth went soft against his. He helped her off with her underthings, as she always left him to do, and from there, things took their course as they should in a darkened bedroom.

While he was still looking down at her, into her sparkling eyes, she smiled and said, "Let's eat lunch at Taco John's."

He withdrew and scooted onto his side, leaning on his left elbow. "You mean go back into town?"

"I'm hungry for fake Mexican food."

"O.K." He had had it in mind to cook bacon and eggs, brew a pot of coffee, and maybe listen to a tape. She was always willing to let him cook. But now the plan had changed. It would be tacos and beer instead. He rolled over to the edge of the bed, toward the window. "Let me check and see where they're getting with that fire."

The fire truck had made its way to the biggest part of the blaze, and the crew was pouring a stream of water at it, an arc of bright water that crested and fell in a spray on the flames.

Clay let his eyes rove across the countryside. The pale colors of winter covered it—the muted tans and greys of the plains country. A field of corn stubble verged toward a pale yellow, and the sagebrush in his own horse pasture showed clumps of the silver green, but overall the country was like a coyote hide, flecked here and there but all of one piece.

The cattails, bull thistles, and water grasses, all winter-dead, were turning to flame. The fire truck was crawling along eastward with the fire, its lone nozzle working hard against wind and fuel. That was how firemen saw it, how he had heard them talk about it. Grass, brush, and timber were all fuel. "If it was ever alive, it'll burn," they said.

Clay looked a quarter mile to the east, to a stand of elm trees on the opposite bank. Large broken-off branches hung down into the tall grass, where, as he knew from hunting pheasants along the drainage, there was plenty of deadfall. He thought the fire would make it to the trees.

He glanced at Cindy. She was sitting on the edge of the bed. She had hooked her bra together and was shifting it around so that the cups would be in front.

Clay faced the window again. Two more fire trucks were pulling into the pasture where the first one had entered. He felt relieved. Now he wouldn't have to feel guilty about not going down there with a shovel and a wet burlap sack.

"Here come two more fire trucks," he said. "That should help."

"What do you think started it?" Cindy was standing up now, adjusting her bra.

"Looks like Mace was burning weeds. There was no wind when we left for church. But he ought to know it picks up at around ten or eleven this time of year."

"He probably feels pretty dumb right now, if he's the one who started it."

"It'll cost him a few cases of beer, you can bet that."

"Oh?"

"That's how volunteer firemen get paid."

"It's the least he could do. I'd think they deserve it," she said.

"Oh, they earn it."

Clay and Cindy got into her silver Sunbird. Clay drove. Cindy lit a cigarette. As they left the tear-shaped driveway to turn north, he looked again down into the bottom. Two fire trucks were fighting the main fire, and the third one was spraying along the fenceline. The fire chief's white Suburban was parked safely in the middle of the pasture.

When they came home with the tacos, the fire had made it to the elm trees, and all three fire trucks were spraying at the blaze. Firemen were also scattered back along the levee, shovelling dirt on little pocket fires. Across the valley, pickups were parked along the county road, becoming part of the spectacle.

Cindy, who had shown little interest in the fire, set the warm bag of tacos on the dining room table. The fire was out of view from there. Clay brought two cans of Coors from the refrigerator.

"What are you going to do this afternoon?" she asked.

"Originally I was going to ride the horse, but with all the commotion down there, I think I'll just bring her in and give her a brushing."

"Uh-huh."

"How about you?"

"I need to call my mom. Then I might even read for a while."

"Uh-huh."

Clay unwrapped his first taco and bit into it. That was the way Sundays seemed to go. He had quit asking her to do things with him, like take a walk down to the bottom or look for pincushion cactus. If he watched football, she did her nails and worked on a crossword puzzle in her sewing room. If he lifted weights in the basement, she watched television upstairs. If he worked outside, she worked inside or watched television.

They ate the lunch without saying much. Clay finished his beer and said, "I'll do the dishes." He stuffed the napkins and wrappers into the paper bag, crushed it all into a ball, and pushed away from the table. She glanced up at him without raising her head, and he realized he hadn't made it sound enough like a joke.

She lit a cigarette. "Thanks, honey."

He leaned to kiss her, and he got some of the taste of the cigarette.

Miss Kitty was a dark nine-year-old mare, the color of the darkest pipe tobacco but not a true black. As he brushed her, shreds of hair came off in the flat, rubber-toothed brush. In another month or so, her coat would come off like thatch, but now it lifted off just a few hairs at a stroke. He combed her mane and tail, ran his hand the length of her underside, checked her hooves, and massaged the skull at the base of her ears. When he was done, he turned her back into the pasture.

Down in the bottom, where he and Miss Kitty usually took their ride, the firefighters were still at it. He was sure he knew some of them, but he avoided looking in their direction. He still felt a twinge of guilt that he should have gone down to help.

Clay went to the tack shed for a can of rolled oats. He crawled through the strands of the barbed wire fence and poured the oats into the feed box next to the horse tank. He patted Miss Kitty's neck as she pushed her nose into the oats. She came up with a mouthful, with loose oats scattering to the ground. As she worked her mouth, a few more dry flakes fell, and, caught by the breeze, landed in the water trough. Stepping toward her so that she hung her head over his left shoulder, he patted her neck with his flat hand. Then he moved away, rubbed the back of his first two fingers against her velvet nose, and took the grain can to the shed.

Cindy was watching a movie when he went into the house. He stood by her chair, gazing at the television without any interest, until she said, "Yes?"

"I was wondering if there was anything you'd like to have done. I put the horse away."

"It didn't take you long."

"Nah, I just brushed her down and put her away."

Cindy waited a few seconds and said, "There's that chair that needs to be fixed. The recliner."

"Oh."

"You don't have to."

"Well, it needs to be done sometime."

"If there's something else you'd rather be doing—"

"No, that's all right. I've got the time. I can do it."

"Honey, why don't you do something fun?"

"Oh, I did. It just didn't take long. So I thought I could get something else done. That chair has been sitting there long enough, anyway."

She glanced away from the television, reached for his hand, and squeezed it.

Clay went to the basement and wrestled the recliner into the middle of the exercise area. One of the rivets had broken on the accordion hinge, so he would have to drill it out and put in a small stove bolt and nut. He wouldn't be able to tighten it all the way, so he would have to keep an eye on it from then on, to see if the nut worked its way loose. Clay didn't like this sort of work to begin with, and he knew a makeshift job when he did one, but if it worked they had a recliner again.

The whole job took about an hour, including sweeping up the metal grains and putting the tools away. The chair flopped back and forth just fine, with or without him sitting in it. He carried the recliner up the stairs and set it in the living room. Cindy had just turned off the television.

She swiped two fingers across the vinyl arm. "It got dusty down there. I'll have to clean it off." She turned to Clay and kissed him. "Thanks, honey." Clay got a taste of cigarette again.

He went out the back door and over to the corner of the yard. Smoke was still rising in wisps along the slough, but the fire had been put out and the trucks were gone. The banks had been burned off on both sides of the drainage. Most of the land on either side had been disked or plowed in the fall, but in those places where there was grass, side fires had eaten black patches away from the bank. Some of those spots were smoking, as was the ravaged stand of elms. From this distance, it looked as if some of the live growth in those trees had taken a pretty good burning.

The sun had moved into the west. He had a little more than an hour left in the afternoon, time for some small chore. He wandered to the front yard, where he saw, as he had seen without thinking when he grained the horse, that last year's lilac blossoms needed to be cut out. He went to the garage and found his pair of hand shears and a five-gallon bucket.

The old lilac blooms were dry and brown, with dead pods like flat wooden grapes. Each cluster, or bunch, grew out from the center of a "V" formed by first-year growth. The dead blooms looked ugly when the bushes were leafless, so he cut them, one by one, leaving a clean "V" each time.

The sun was slipping into the hills when he finished. He put the shears into the pocket of his canvas chore coat, and he carried the light, dry load to the gully west of the house. There he emptied the bucket onto the heap where in the past he had tossed cactus, sand burrs, puncture vines, and stray clippings.

On his way back to the garage, he heard a whiffling sound overhead. Pausing in the driveway, he raised his eyes to the sky. A half-dozen ducks were flying over, the quick beat of their wings whistling. After putting away the bucket and the shears, he returned to stand in the driveway.

The kitchen light was on, and Clay remembered he was supposed to skin the chicken so Cindy could season it and roast it. That task could wait a few minutes longer. He would take this bit of time for himself, these few minutes that might be the best he would know today.

The sunset was spreading scarves of peach and fuchsia in the southwestern sky. The breeze was softer now, as it often was at dusk. He could catch a trace of the burnt smell; most of it would be wafted off to the east, down below. Here on the hill, the evening was cool and clear. The smell of the smoke reminded him of kissing Cindy. There had been a time when he hadn't noticed the smoking or any of her other ways that now irritated him. He didn't like to admit it, but maybe the best part of their life together had already burned itself out, without their doing much about it.

Clay found the gloves in the left pocket of his coat, and he put them on. He stood in the driveway, off to one side of the light from the kitchen window. The felt hat, quilted coat, and lined gloves kept him warm in the cooling air.

A squeaking in the sky made him look up. A flock of geese was flying in the same direction as the ducks had gone, from the reservoirs and grain stubble in the south to wherever they bedded down for the night. Against the sky, which was fading grey, their firm, sleek bodies moved as the wings flapped. Geese moved their wings half as fast as ducks did. Clay heard the slow swish of their wings, the wheezing honk as they called back and forth in their soaring "V."

Sometimes in the afternoon they dropped into the corn stubble down below, and their cackling and clamoring would carry up on the cool air. Today, of course, they hadn't been there. Some days they were, and some days they weren't. But this was the best of it anyway, when he could feel like a boy in his hat and gloves and chore coat, leaning back and looking up as the wild geese flew overhead, caressing the first dark skies of the night.

All Our Neighbors Have Blue Lights

There's a turkey carcass in the refrigerator, wrapped up in aluminum foil. From out here on the porch, I can see it clearly, in my mind. It's not picked all the way clean. I could chip off enough meat for a few decent sandwiches, or I could take it apart to make soup, or I could do both. The way I feel right now, I could throw the damn thing away, tell Wendy it was dried out and starting to smell sour, and then leave it up to her to put together dinner.

All I really wanted, this time, was a nice house for her to come home to. And it's not nice, not now. I really feel like throwing out the turkey, saying hell with it, you get dinner.

I thought I had everything in good order. I was figuring our bills and expenses when she came home from the weekend conference. She dropped her bags right inside the door, let out a deep breath, and came over to give me a kiss as I sat at the desk.

"Whatcha doin'?"

"Bills."

"Um."

"Would you do me a favor and get me a beer, please?"

"Sure." It worked. When she went to the refrigerator and opened it, she let out a two-syllable "Oh-oo." She brought me the beer and kissed me again. "You defrosted the refrigerator."

I stood up, away from the desk. "And that's not all." I sipped on my beer. "How was your conference?"

"Oh, it was all right. What else did you do around the house?" She stepped back into the kitchen. "O.K. You cleaned the top of the stove. And the top of the refrigerator. You mopped the floor." She came back to the living room. "You dusted." I followed her down the hallway. She peeked into the extra bedroom.

"Nothing in there," I said.

"Oh, O.K." She flicked on the bathroom light and looked in. "You cleaned the bathroom. You dear. That's ten extra points."

I was glowing by now, as she paused at the bedroom doorway. Standing behind her, I slipped my free right hand around her waist and kissed her on the neck.

"You made the bed."

"Uh-huh. I even changed the sheets and did the laundry."

I was going to set my beer on the dresser, then tumble her into that bed with the clean sheets, when she stiffened and turned toward me.

"Why did you do that?"

"I wanted to have a nice house for you to come home to."

"But you never do that. You don't ever change the sheets or wash them."

"I guess I was just on a cleaning spree."

"Did you have somebody over?"

"What?"

"Did you have company?"

"Hell, no, I didn't have company. I just felt like doing some house work. Apparently more than I should have bothered with." We were standing apart by now, so I took my beer back to my desk. She didn't say anything as she picked up her bags and carried them to the bedroom. As I finished with the bills, I heard her putting her things away. The suitcases went *clunk* as she stacked them in her closet.

* * * * *

She's in the shower now, and I'm out here on the porch with my second beer. I want her to have her own line of work. It means a lot to her, and it helps us have the things we'd like to have. We're not rich. We don't have a self-defrosting refrigerator or a self-cleaning oven or a satellite dish like most of our neighbors do, but we have our own place, this one-level, three-bedroom house on five acres, with a horse barn. Her horse barn, really, but that's O.K.

I think I know more about marriage than I'm willing to let on, even to my wife. I want her to have her own career to develop, even though I have a notion of who was at the conference and how some of the rooming might have gone on. Maybe that's why she took the line she did—the best defense is a good offense. Maybe that's why she's in the shower.

I didn't have anybody over this time, but maybe I should have if I'm going to take the blame for it. No, that's a cheap thought, thinking of how to get even. Maybe I'm getting the treatment now for what I got away with before. Or thought I did. It's just coming around now.

She'll be on the lookout for the next few days— probably have an eye out for a dropped earring or a cigarette stub. There won't be any. She'll have a casual question slipped in here and there, but they'll be easy questions to answer. No, there were no phone calls the whole weekend. Yes, it cooled down at night; I had to pull the blanket over me. Yes, I had time to catch the horse and put fly spray on him.

The sun is going down. We've had the longest day of the year, and already the days are getting shorter and the sunsets are moving south, tree by tree above the windbreak to the west. The clouds are red orange, the color of that one bunch of tulips that bloomed in May.

I'm mad now, probably defensive in some ways, but I know that deep down, I care more for my wife than I've made clear to her today. I remember one day I stopped at the store to buy milk. The girl at the checkstand, Dottie, told me that Wendy had just been in to buy milk. So I left the milk there, and on the way home I saw a wreck. Straight ahead of me, sideways in the middle of the road, a car was tipped over so that all I could see was the underside. Parallel with it, on the pavement ahead of me, was a half-gallon of milk—our brand. Instead of driving around as the cop waved me to do, I pulled over to the shoulder.

There was a bashed-up pickup nose-down in the ditch on my right as I ran around the tipped-over car. Then I saw that it wasn't her car at all; it was a car I didn't recognize. Everyone was talking about how it had happened, and the police radio was squawking. A cop stood in front of me and listened to my disconnected explanation of how I'd thought it was my wife's car but it wasn't. He called me son, told me no one was hurt very badly. He said they were waiting for the wrecker.

The milk was in the refrigerator when I got home.

That incident scared the hell out of me, and it made me realize how much I didn't want to lose her. And still, I let this little conflict about the sheets sneak up on us.

Maybe we'll go out for dinner. I'll just leave that turkey in there, wrapped in foil. It won't dry out or spoil in just one day.

* * * * *

We went out for dinner, to a little family restaurant that had humorous paper place mats. The humor dwelled upon the things it took to be a rancher—a pickup with a gun rack in front and a dog in back, a wife with a good job at the courthouse, and that sort of thing. Since I'm the one with the job at the courthouse and she's the one who has the horse, I didn't find the place mats all that hilarious. But we had an agreeable meal. We both had chicken.

The neighbors have apparently all gone to bed. The house lights are all out, and each place is represented by a little blue light—one of those yard lanterns that zap bugs. In the daytime I can sit here and see their satellite dishes, like four huge petunias in a row. Now it's as if the satellite dishes have all shrunken, drawn in to a small glowing center, as if the flowers have closed up for the night.

Four lights in a row, blue as the bachelor buttons blooming now in the garden. From the outside, all our neighbors look the same—mediocre, content, probably happy. From here a person could almost believe that each family shut off the television, caught that soft glow of complacency in a globe lantern, and hung it out for the night as a token of assurance.

I can visualize Wendy right now, sitting up in bed with the light on, reading *The Clan of the Cave Bear* or *The Mammoth Hunters*, whichever one she is on now. I can also imagine the turkey carcass, next to the carton of milk in the inside dark of the refrigerator.

Earlier in the evening I felt that I'd been picked pretty clean myself, but now in the safe softness of night I feel the flesh of life coming back. It reminds me of a hand-dug well on the farm I grew up on. It had a hand pump, and every once in a while it would just quit coughing up water. We would leave it alone for a few days, and water would seep back into it. That was a good well. It probably has water in it right now.

It would seem that behind those blue lights everyone is sleeping well, that fathers and mothers went to bed pleased with their children, pleased by one another as husband and wife. It would be nice to think that everyone else is the same, that we are the only ones on our road who go to bed with uncertainties or misgivings. We hang our blue sheets on the clothesline to wave at our neighbors, who in turn must suppose we are happy. As we pass on the road they wave to us as we wave to them, good neighbors all.

It's time now to go to bed myself, to join my wife. The fresh sheets will feel good on a summer night like this. If a neighbor happens to be sitting sleepless on his porch, I hope he is comforted to see our light, the last bright restless light on our road, wink out.

About the Author

John D. Nesbitt lives in the plains country of Wyoming, where he teaches English and Spanish at Eastern Wyoming College. His articles, reviews, fiction, and poetry have appeared in numerous magazines and anthologies. He has had more than thirty books published, including short story collections, contemporary novels, and traditional westerns, as well as textbooks for his courses. John has won many awards for his work, including two awards from the Wyoming State Historical Society (for fiction), two awards from Wyoming Writers for encouragement of other writers and service to the organization, two Wyoming Arts Council literary fellowships (one for fiction, one for non-fiction), a Will Rogers Medallion Award for *Dark Prairie* (a frontier mystery) and another for *Thorns on the Rose* (a poetry collection), a Western Writers of America Spur finalist award for his novel *Raven Springs*, and the Spur award itself for his short story "At the End of the Orchard" and for his novels *Trouble at the Redstone* and *Stranger in Thunder Basin*. His recent work includes *Poacher's Moon*, a contemporary novel; *Blue Horse Mesa*, a collection of western stories; and *Field Work*, a retro-noir fiction collection. Visit his website at www.johndnesbitt.com

"NESBITT IS A TRUE ARTIST."
—WESTERN AMERICAN LITERATURE

John D. Nesbitt

TWO NOVELLAS

Published by SpeakingVolumes

Visit us at www.speakingvolumes.us

John D. Nesbitt

NotARustler

"NESBITT IS A TRUE ARTIST."
—WESTERN AMERICAN LITERATURE

Published by SpeakingVolumes

Visit us at www.speakingvolumes.us

John D. Nesbitt

POACHER'S
MOON

"NESBITT IS A TRUE ARTIST."
—WESTERN AMERICAN LITERATURE

Published by SpeakingVolumes

Visit us at www.speakingvolumes.us

John D. Nesbitt

MAN FROM
WOLF RIVER

"NESBITT IS A TRUE ARTIST."
—WESTERN AMERICAN LITERATURE

Published by SpeakingVolumes

Visit us at www.speakingvolumes.us

Visit us at <u>www.speakingvolumes.us</u>

FOR MORE EXCITING BOOKS, E-BOOKS, AUDIOBOOKS AND MORE

visit us at
www.speakingvolumes.us

Sign up for free and bargain books

Join the Speaking Volumes mailing list

Text

ILOVEBOOKS
to 22828 to get started.

Message and data rates may apply.

www.ingramcontent.com/pod-product-compliance
Lightning Source LLC
Chambersburg PA
CBHW020613250626
47154CB00004B/1485